ISLAND FEVER

KATE ASTER

PROLOGUE

ONE MONTH AGO

- DODGER -

"Did you know that Ariana Grande has a pet pig?"

There are moments when I feel the sting of being single again more than others. Right now, as I contemplate my date's question while the sun sets on the Ko Olina lagoon where my brother just took his marital vows, I'm definitely having one of those moments.

"I'm sorry—what?" I ask my date.

"Did you know that Ariana Grande has a pet pig?"

I stare at Leona, who all but sparkles in her frosted lips and shimmering highlighted hair that cascades down her back. I have no idea who Ariana Grande is. I'm sure I've heard the name before, but my first guess would be that it's a new coffee they offer at Starbucks.

Of course, I'm not foolish enough to say that. "I didn't know that," I tell her instead.

"His name is Piggy Smallz."

"Ah, interesting choice for a name." I reach for my drink and take a few generous gulps. I should ask her to dance again. She's a good dancer—a conclusion that I truly would have drawn for myself even if she hadn't told me multiple times tonight. She definitely hits the O'ahu nightclub scene regularly. And the best thing about her dancing is that she doesn't talk at the same time.

It's not her fault. It's my own. I was foolish enough to actually take a blind date to my brother Fen's wedding. I know—for a guy who graduated at the top of his class in medical school, I'm not feeling like the sharpest knife in the drawer right now.

Only a month has passed since my girlfriend Hailey left Hawai'i, so I didn't have any problem going stag to this event.

But then I heard a few of my Ohio cousins were making the trek to O'ahu to see my brother get hitched, too. Logan, Ryan, and Dylan are all married. Toss in the fact that both my brothers are married now, and I could foresee myself spending the entire evening hearing their theories about why I'm still single.

So when a doc I work with at my urgent care center on the Big Island told me his sister was on O'ahu and would love go with me, I was foolish enough to figure, why the hell not?

"Would you believe he has 569,000 Instagram followers?" she asks.

"No. No, that's definitely surprising."

"And he barely ever posts anything. But he's *still* got that many followers."

My head cocks as I gaze at her. "I'm trying to figure out

how a pig managed to post anything. No opposable thumbs, you know. It would make holding a phone difficult."

She giggles uproariously and as one of my cousins passes with his wife on his arm, he sends me a sympathetic look.

"You sound like such a doctor when you say things like that." Her eyes light at the mention of my profession.

"That's probably because I am one."

"And you were in the Army, too," she says, as though I needed reminding. "Is it true that you got a Purple Heart?"

"No. I got a Bronze Star."

She looks disappointed. "What did you do to get that?"

"I, uh, exposed myself to enemy fire to treat some Soldiers in the field." I don't go into specifics because it always sounds like I'm trying to impress people. And I hate that, because all I was doing was my job. I was there to care for the wounded. It doesn't matter if they're in a combat zone or at Dairy Queen.

"And they didn't give you a Purple Heart?"

"No. They only do that if you get wounded. I managed to duck at just the right times."

She looks crestfallen, so much so that I almost point out that the Bronze Star ranks higher than a Purple Heart.

But she stops me by saying, "Too bad. I like purple."

I swallow a laugh. Really, if either of my brothers heard this conversation, it would be reenacted every time we had a barbeque.

Suddenly, her brow rises and a smile spreads as she pulls her phone off the table... again. Sliding toward me, she exclaims, "Selfie!" and snaps a picture that she promptly posts online.

"That photo can't be different from the one you posted five minutes ago," I can't help noting.

Her eyes widen considerably. "Oh, there's a lot more to it than that. There's a science to posting. I have to keep posting or I lose followers. I have more than two thousand. I'm trying to get it to ten thousand by the end of the year."

"That's an ambitious goal," I respond with complete sincerity. Even though I have no clue about social media and hired a consultant to handle it for my clinic, I can appreciate to some degree her interest in it. Frankly, it's the most interesting thing she's said all night. "Maybe one day you'll have more than Piggy Smallz."

"I hope so. You know what I wonder about him?"

I can't imagine. "No. What?"

"I wonder if he knows he's so famous. You know? I mean, he's just a pig."

I nod stoically, mildly optimistic that at least *she* knows he's just a pig. "The only thing I wonder about Piggy Smallz is how much bacon I could get out of him," I joke.

A look of horror washes over her face and she sucks in a sharp breath. "That's offensive. I'm vegetarian!"

Well, shit. "I'm sorry. I was just kidding."

"I think it's horrible that you'd even *think* about eating someone's pet."

I look at the way her eyes are slicing me to bits and her fingers curl around her drink, and I can't help thinking that I survived deployments, got a Bronze Star, just sold my first franchise of the urgent care center I started... and yet I'll be remembered this way, as the guy who is about to be stabbed with the stem of a champagne glass by his date. "I really wasn't considering *doing* it. It was just a joke. Tasteless." There's this part of me that wants to say something like how it's been at least a year since I've eaten someone's pet. But I'm getting the impression she doesn't like the Sheridan brand of humor. "Really. My apologies. And as a doctor, I applaud that you're a vegetarian."

She looks mildly placated. "Fish is so much better anyway."

"Technically, then, I guess you're a pescatarian."

She shakes her head. "No. I don't really believe in religion."

My mouth opens to tell her that a pescatarian is someone who eats fish, but not other meat. But I snap it shut, finally learning that every time I speak around this woman, I tend to regret it.

Instead, I avert my eyes to my brother in the distance, holding his gorgeous bride tightly in his arms as they sway to Hawaiian music. It was a perfect beachside ceremony. A perfect reception. A perfect starlit night on the Ko Olina lagoon on their new island home of O'ahu.

This is the night that my brothers and I had the joy and privilege of welcoming Kaila into our fold. She is a Sheridan now, God help her.

Yet I'll likely remember this wedding as the night I learned about Piggy Smallz.

CHAPTER 1

ONE MONTH LATER

- DODGER -

I blame AP Biology.

That's generally the first thing I think when my phone rings at some late hour with an emergency that just can't wait until dawn.

When I started the urgent care center in Waikoloa on the Big Island of Hawai'i, I thought I had said good-bye to the late nights of being an on-call doctor. After I leave our clinic off Mauna Lani Drive, my time is my own.

But not tonight.

Tonight I got a call from my brother telling me that my precious niece is running a pretty impressive fever and their pediatrician isn't returning their calls. So right now, rather than blaming AP Biology for pulling me away from my date, I'm just damn grateful to be a doctor so I can help out.

Truth is, I might have chosen this path for myself even if it hadn't been for that A that I'd earned so easily in AP Bio long ago; even if my father hadn't seen that score on my report card and started kicking me down the straight and narrow path that led to medical school.

Looking back, I guess I didn't show much of a backbone. But I was young to be a freshman in high school, having skipped a grade. And my backbone didn't form completely till I joined the Army—a move that got me my medical degree on Uncle Sam's dime.

The Army has a way of taking a spineless kid and helping him grow himself a good, strong backbone. Then they generally test the hell out of it by throwing a 45-pound rucksack on his back or telling him he's got to jump out of a Chinook at twelve hundred feet, or any of the numerous ways military life can destroy the human body.

But if I didn't get that A in AP Bio—if my dad hadn't "coaxed" me (his word, not mine) down this path when I'd been too young to put up a fight—then I wouldn't be here in my brother's house able to save him and his wife a scary trip to the ER.

"It's just a cold," I tell them after I listen to their baby's lungs. I don't bother hiding the relief in my own voice. After all, she's my only niece and I'm wrapped around her tiny finger.

Camden is sheet-white and considering the guy used to be an Army Ranger, it's almost laughable how a few digits on a thermometer can bring him this amount of terror.

But that's parenthood for you. I've seen it in countless people in my business. And maybe if I could ever find a woman who didn't leave this island as quickly as she sets foot on it, I might experience it myself one day.

"Just a cold?" Annie verifies. She's every bit as pale as Cam. But that's the norm for her.

"Lungs are clear and it's not the flu. The most important thing you can do is just keep her resting and hydrated."

"So this is… nothing to worry about?"

"Well, she's still a baby," I remind them. "They're fragile at this age. So I'll come over and check on her first thing tomorrow morning—make sure those lungs are still clear. And we'll get that fever headed in the right direction. But I want you to call her pediatrician again as soon as they open up in the morning."

Cam's frown deepens. "Yeah, I'll call him. And I'll ask him why after three calls to their after-hours number I'm still waiting for a call back."

"Mind texting me their number?" I ask. I think I'd like to have a little come-to-Jesus talk with this pediatrician and figure out whether my niece needs to find a new one.

Trouble is, there just aren't many on this rock.

"Sure. Thanks again for coming. I just was worried about taking her to the ER for what would probably be a three-hour wait."

"Don't worry about it. You did the right thing." I drape my stethoscope over my neck and pick up Baby K—a nickname we gave their child because naming her after her Aunt Kaila has made life pretty damn confusing around here. "Most important thing is to rest. Not just her—you guys, too."

Cam gives a stubborn shake of his head. "I don't need sleep. I'll stay up and keep an eye on her."

I have to fight the urge to roll my eyes. My younger brother is as predictable as a fart after chili, an adage he proudly came up with himself and is still hoping will catch on.

"This thing's been going around like wildfire," I advise him. "I've seen at least ten cases of it since last week. If you don't get some sleep, I can pretty much guarantee you'll be the next one to get sick."

I watch Annie rest her hand on Cam's forearm. "I'll make sure he gets some rest."

"And you, too, Annie."

"I will—*oh no!*" Her face screws up suddenly and she looks at Cam with panic.

"What?" I glance between the two of them.

"We've got company coming."

I cock my head slightly. We live in the middle of the Pacific. And even though people say they're going to take advantage of the offer of a free place to stay in Hawai'i, they generally balk when they see the hefty price of a plane ticket.

I dart my eyes to Cam. "Family?" I can't recall Mom or Dad saying they were coming out at this time of year. But I imagine since I'm not the one who managed to produce an adorable grandchild for our parents, they might have cut me out of the conversation.

"No. Annie's friend Sam. You remember her—she came out for Baby K's baptism?"

Samantha. Yeah, I remember her and her boyfriend. Carl... or something like that. I couldn't pick either one of them out of a line-up. All I saw was the tops of their heads because they pretty much spent their entire visit looking at their phones.

"You should probably cancel," I suggest. "You need your rest, and you won't be doing anyone any favors by exposing her to this."

Annie's shoulders sag and she glances at her watch. "She's on a plane now. She's arriving tomorrow."

I stiffen, the protective uncle in me rearing his ugly head. "Well, Baby K's immune system's working hard enough. No need to pass her into the arms of someone who's been enjoying recirculated air on a plane." I'm not paranoid about germs, even though my brothers will say otherwise. I couldn't survive as a doctor if I was. But I've seen that recirculated air ruin too many once-in-a-lifetime vacations to Hawai'i. I know this because they all end up in my waiting room with their fevers and body aches.

"Oh, God." Annie looks deflated. "I feel so bad. I'll see if I can find a hotel that's not filled."

I wince. Sure, hotels here will have an open room, but they'll make you pay dearly for a last-minute reservation. "Look, just have her stay with me. She's got her choice of extra bedrooms. There's a pool. I'm right on the beach. You're not going to do better than that unless she wants to pay $600 a night."

"You really wouldn't mind?"

I shrug. I imagine Samantha will be on her phone the entire time, so I doubt she'll be looking for me to entertain her. She'll hole-up in one of the rooms and carry on business as though she never left DC. I know her type well—I used to be one of them.

Besides, I'd do just about anything to make my sister-in-law look a little less overwhelmed right now. "Don't mind at all. Unless you think that boyfriend of hers would mind." I'm only half joking. Guys sometimes get a little threatened when they see me walk into the room. But my guess is that Carl guy would only be threatened if I grabbed his phone and held it over the deep end of a pool.

"I doubt Carl would mind." She sighs. "I don't think he cares much about anything except his phone."

Phew. At least I'm not the only one thinking it. "What time does her flight come in?"

Annie gives me the flight details and I check on Baby K one last time before Cam walks me to my car.

"Thanks for coming out so fast, Bro." He thumps me on my back when we reach my car. "I feel bad, cutting your date short like that."

I swing open the door to my Jeep. "You did me a favor."

"That bad?"

I bristle slightly. I don't like talking trash about women. It takes all kinds to keep this world spinning. But there's no denying I've had some regrettable dates since Hailey left the island a couple months ago. "Well, she had her good points. But I knew I was in for a rough night when she told me she gets all of her news from things her friends share on Facebook. She actually believes some viral story about a swimmer in 'Ewa Beach who inhaled a fish egg and it grew inside her lung until she coughed out a live angelfish months later."

He laughs. "Doesn't sound like the right fit for a scientific guy like you."

"I could get past that," I admit, knowing that I'm on an island and the pickings are slim. People come and go like the tides here, so those of us who stick around have learned to value friendships with people you'd never hang out with on the mainland. It's actually a pretty enlightened way to live a life. "A lot of people fall for things they see online. But she practically got combative when I told her it was impossible for an angelfish to incubate and survive inside a human body."

"Well, I see her point. You're only a doctor. And we're talking Facebook here, a highly credible news source." His sarcasm fades and he looks sympathetic as I climb into my Jeep. "Why are people always setting you up with bad dates, Bro? And more importantly, why are you letting them?"

I fight the urge to glare at my brother. He's tired. He's worried about his baby. He's been married for just long enough that he's forgotten what it's like to be single on an island. "Hey, do I have to remind you that you married your babysitter?"

"Oh. Yeah, I guess I forgot what it's like out there. The bar scene here has nothing but tourists. How about just not trying to find *anyone* and let destiny do it for you?"

I roll my eyes. "Destiny is a concept sold to us by Hollywood," I tell him. For me, dating is more of a numbers game. If you date enough, you are increasing your chances of finding a sufficient mate. Which is why I've got another date lined up for later this week. But I hold back telling my brother that. "You've been watching too many chick flicks with Annie."

He nods. "I won't dispute that Netflix is killing me. I mean, as if it wasn't enough that I had to watch *Mama Mia!*, then I find out there's a damn sequel. Why do I have to watch this stuff?"

"Because your wife went through childbirth, so that gives her the power of the remote control for at least three more years in my book. Suck it up, Soldier."

"Yeah, no kidding."

"Call me if Baby K gets any worse, Cam. Don't hesitate. She's my only niece. You can't screw her up."

He chuckles as he steps away from my car and I pull away.

When I get back to the three-bedroom condo on the water I used to share with my brothers, it seems emptier to me after seeing Cam's home up in Waikoloa Village. His is strewn with baby toys and swings and the scent of dirty diapers even though they bought one of those special trash cans that's supposed to eliminate the smell.

Now that Fen is newly married, I picture the home he shares with Kaila on O'ahu will likely look the same as Cam's in a year or two.

I open the windows in my bedroom so that I can hear the

surf breaking in the ocean just steps from my condo. When I set my phone next to my bedside. I leave the ringer on just in case Baby K takes a turn for the worse. Then I close my eyes and let sleep tug me downward.

Just as I'm drifting, an image comes to mind—the way that chestnut brown hair of Samantha's draped gently over her conservative aquamarine dress she wore to Baby K's baptism. I stood beside her in the church that day; Annie made Samantha her child's godmother and I was honored to be named godfather, probably more out of sympathy seeing as I'm the only unmarried brother and they might be wondering if I'll ever even have kids of my own.

Samantha.

I was with Hailey back then. And when I'm in a relationship with a woman, my eyes don't stray. So I barely glanced at Samantha that day.

But maybe I *did* notice a little more about her than just the top of her head, as I had told Cam earlier tonight.

And maybe this might be a little more challenging than I thought.

CHAPTER 2

~ SAMANTHA ~

Long-distance travel never bothers me.

Never, until about thirty seconds ago.

When I worked for the firm, I did plenty of it, generally traveling around the country to visit members of Congress in their home states. Meeting with them "outside the beltway," as we say in DC, was a great way to build stronger relationships.

So the two-hour flight from DC to Atlanta was as easy as taking a breath. And even the ten-hour connecting flight that I'm on now, headed to my final destination in the middle of the Pacific, doesn't make me blink twice.

Hell, I can even receive texts in the air these days, even though the in-flight app I use isn't quite as efficient as I'd get when I'm on the ground. Not efficient at all, actually, as I've just confirmed when I receive a text that appears to have been sent hours ago.

"Baby K's sick," Annie had written. And that's about all it takes for me to be nearly begging the flight attendant for one of those tiny bottles of wine.

That's it. Just a few words... and the little bubble displaying a few dots telling me that another text is trying to come through, but seems to be stuck in cyberspace.

Stupid in-flight texting app.

The remainder of the flight is nothing short of painful.

Baby K's sick.

Baby K—whom I prefer to call Kaila because she'll hate that nickname when she's older—is my beloved goddaughter and the most important thing in my life right now.

Which is why my gut has twisted into a knot.

I restart my phone, hoping that might help the text arrive, but to no avail.

So, for the rest of the flight, I find myself feeling a bit like a caged animal more than I normally would in the confines of a plane.

Times like these, I regret encouraging my friend to settle down on an island in the middle of the Pacific more than 4,500 miles away from me. It's been hard keeping in touch, especially with her getting into a routine of mommy groups, and me, struggling to make myself irreplaceable at Trenton, Leopold, and Wagner—a task at which I apparently failed.

When little Kaila was born, I managed to make it out to Hawai'i for her baptism—even at the risk of seeming dispensable at work. How could I not? Never in my life have I cried happy tears—I'm just not the type—except for the day that Annie told me she wanted me to be her baby's godmother.

Then I got the promotion I'd dreamed of since I had started at the firm, and I wasn't sure when I'd get the chance to see the baby again.

The moment we touch down, my phone is in a death grip as I finally see a flurry of texts pour in.

"Baby K's sick," I see again.

Then the next words bring me some comfort. "Dodger says it's just a cold, but we r a mess over here and really need 2 get some sleep. SO SORRY but I don't think we r up 4 a guest right now."

Her child is sick and she's worried about me? That's so like Annie, and I'm not sure if I want to strangle her for it or hug her. I've missed my friend.

"Dodger's going 2 pick u up. He's got your flight info," she continues. "Says u can stay w/ him. Do u mind?"

To my dying day, I'll deny the flurry of butterflies I feel in my stomach at the thought of sharing a place with Dodger.

I'm even perplexed a moment, as I just met Dodger's girl-friend Hailey at the baptism almost a year ago. I know they're still a pair. Earlier this year, Annie joked that modeling agencies were already lining up to represent Dodger and Hailey's future children; the two of them look *that* gorgeous together.

I liked Hailey. We talked a little after the baptism in those rare moments when my phone wasn't bugging me with work calls and texts. She lives on the other side of the island working as a geologist, close to where the volcano is, I'd gathered. But they somehow manage to make their relation-ship work.

Hailey is one of those perfect people that you can't resist hoping will be somehow flawed. Yet she's not. And by the end of a conversation with her, you figure that's okay, too.

My first thought is whether she'd somehow mind my sharing a roof with Dodger for a few nights until little Kaila is better. Then I pull out my compact to wipe away the remains of yesterday's mascara that are smeared under my eyes. And I'm reminded that a woman who looks like a model for one of those fitness wear catalogs would definitely not see me as any kind of threat.

As people start to stand to retrieve their luggage from the overhead compartments, I tap in a text. "Don't worry about it. Glad it's just a cold. That's got 2 b scary. Now turn your phone off and get a nap if u can. I'll be fine."

And I will. It's not like arriving alone someplace far from home is that new to me. Yet it feels different this time, without work somehow directing every minute of my days ahead.

I tap in a quick text to my mom—no matter how often I travel, she still likes to hear from me when I'm safely on the ground. She replies before I'm even able to slide my phone back into my purse.

"Thx, honey. I really hope your work doesn't mind this time off," it reads. My face falls at her words, not that they're a surprise. She made it pretty clear that she thought it was a mistake to take so much time off work to see my friend and her baby. She frets over my employment status even more than I do, which is exactly why I never told her I was laid off last month.

Her blood pressure likely couldn't take it.

Frowning, I pull my bag out from above me, sling my purse over my shoulder and head up the aisle. People have that frustrated look that they get on a lengthy flight. A baby is wailing and I send the mom a look of sympathy.

The sun strikes my eyes as I step out of the plane onto the ramp. Kona has one of those rare U.S. airports where you step from the plane straight into open air, and I personally hope they never change that. Because the air here—despite the hint of fuel and exhaust scent on the tarmac—is perfumed by saltwater and flowering trees.

If I was anyone else, I'd decompress immediately right

now. Just fill my lungs with the Hawaiian air and feel my blood pressure drop. But I'm not anyone else. I'm me.

I don't decompress very easily or often—not when I was employed by Trenton, Leopold, and Wagner, and certainly not now with no income magically appearing in my bank account every two weeks. A frown touches my lips at the thought. I try to push past it—I haven't told Annie yet that I got laid off.

Truth is, I'd hoped that I would find a job so fast I'd never need to tell anyone. I only told my boyfriend, quickly discovering that was a mistake when he dumped me three days later, apparently finding me less desirable when I'm not gainfully employed.

Bastard.

When I step just past the security gate, I spot Dodger immediately. He's impossible to miss, by far the best looking of the Sheridan brothers, though I'd never tell Annie that. He's the tallest of the three, with tousled, dark hair, shoulders of a linebacker, and a sexy five o'clock shadow on his angular chin.

He eyes me curiously as I approach, probably because he's not sure it's even me. I'm pretty nondescript, especially when I'm not dressed in my DC power suit that makes me feel a hell of a lot more confident than I do in shorts and a t-shirt like I am now.

Watching his apprehensive gaze on me, I lift my hand to send him a wave of assurance. Clearly he noticed me at the baby's baptism as little as my boyfriend did.

Another sucker punch to my ego.

"Hi, Dodger," I say when I'm closer. His smile appears and he extends his hand, holding a flower lei that I failed to notice until now.

"Aloha," he says as he drapes it over my head.

The flowers are intoxicating, yet the lightheadedness I

feel can't be blamed on the glorious aroma. No one has greeted me with flowers before.

Ever.

In two years of dating Carl, never once did he greet me this way. On Valentine's Day, he'd always say how glad he was that I didn't succumb to the pressures of that "made-up holiday." Being me, I was just practical enough not to mind. But now that I've felt that unusual warmth that comes with the smell of flowers that were intended just for me, I'm kind of pissed off that it's taken me this long to experience it.

I touch the orchids lightly. "You didn't have to get me a lei."

"It's a consolation for Annie not being here to pick you up. She feels terrible."

"I wish she wouldn't. I'm just glad that Kaila's going to be okay. She is, right?"

"She'll be fine. I've been checking on her every few hours today. Sick as a dog, but she'll get through it. Cam and Annie might fall apart, though," he adds with a slight laugh.

"Look, it's nice of you to offer to put me up, but I can just grab a room at any hotel."

He shrugs. "I don't mind. I've got the space. Three bedrooms, two vacant, you know. And Annie already dropped off her car at my place so you can use that to get around."

"No. It's too much trouble. I'll just call a hotel and you can drop me off. Where's that place that Annie used to work? The Queen K-something?"

"The Queen Kaʻahumanu Resort? Home of the thirty-dollar omelet?"

"Thirty-dollar omelet?"

"Yep. You really want to go there? They charge you fifteen bucks every time you flush the toilet."

I scoff. "Now I know you're joking."

He smiles. "About that, yes. But not the omelet. Cheapest thing on their menu. Highway robbery."

I nibble my lower lip, thinking. I managed to stash away some money back when I was employed, so I've got a healthy savings account. But the idea of a thirty-dollar omelet is definitely more intimidating when a girl's jobless.

"I don't want things to look—I don't know—weird. You know..." I admit, thinking of Hailey.

"No one would think that," he says. "Unless you think Carl wouldn't like it..." His voice trails.

Carl. A frown threatens. *You mean the same Carl who dumped me three days after I was laid off?* I want to blurt it out. But it's pathetic, really. If I haven't even told Annie yet that Carl dumped me or that I got laid off, I'm not about to blurt out those two juicy tidbits within five minutes of seeing a guy I barely know.

Fact is, I just don't like sympathy. I don't like feeling vulnerable or scared. And to admit it out loud—to actually utter the words, *I got laid off and my boyfriend dumped me because I'm no longer valuable to him without my job*—would somehow make it all that more real to me.

So I reply simply, "Carl won't mind in the slightest," because it's the God's truth.

"Good. Besides, Annie's worried enough right now. She's only going to be more upset if she pictures you forking over a small fortune because her baby is sick."

"Okay." My tone probably sounds more conciliatory than grateful. So I amend quickly with, "This is really nice of you, Dodger. I don't like putting people out like this."

We stop in front of the baggage claim which is already crowded with faces I've come to know over the past ten hours.

"It's really nothing," he answers. "I've got the space. You could live in there for a couple months without me even noticing." He pauses momentarily. "Unless you cook. Because if I actually smelled real food cooking, I'd know something was up."

"I don't cook."

"Then you'll fit into my place just fine. I haven't turned on my oven or stove since I discovered the Foodland up the road from me. Hell of a deli section. Best sushi, *poke*, and *loco moco* on this side of the island."

My face screws up. "You lost me after sushi."

"Don't worry. I'll hook you up." The smile he flashes nearly makes my heart stop. I wonder if Hailey's become immune to it.

I wonder if that's even possible.

I spot my bag as it moves along the conveyor and Dodger retrieves it for me. After he sets it on the ground, I immediately reach for the handle to drag it, and for a moment, his hand is over mine.

My knees instantly turn to mush.

Mouth gaping, I suck in a strangled breath. There should be nothing awkward about this—the feel of his skin on mine for nothing more than a beat or two. Yet my breath is stolen from sensation and I have no idea why.

I'm thirty years old—not some silly schoolgirl. I've shaken the hands of some of the most powerful people in Washington, DC. I've even been in a relationship with a man who did, in fact, close our conversations with an "I love you" at least one out of every ten times when we'd talk.

Yet I've *never* touched a hand and felt weak from the sensation like this. Weak, and yet so alive at the same time.

Holy crap, I need some sleep. That's the only explanation for it. Because that whole I-knew-we-were-destined-for-each-other-when-I-first-touched-him is *so* not my thing.

"I'll take your bag," he says, not removing his hand.

"No, no. I'll get it."

"I insist." He tilts his head. "You look a little pale. Do you want to sit down?"

"No." Embarrassed, I pull my hand from the handle. Then the sensation I feel is almost that of emptiness at the departure of my skin from his. Weird. "I just didn't sleep much on the flight, so technically I've been awake for almost two days now. And thanks," I tack on as I watch him roll my bag.

It's only a short walk to his Jeep—a car that just doesn't quite fit the image I have of him. Back home, a doctor like Dodger would be driving a Mercedes or a BMW at the very least. "You look like you do some off-roading," I say, noting the grime that covers the car as I get inside.

"This is the Big Island. Everyone does some off-roading here. The best beaches aren't accessible any other way."

"Really?"

"Sure. Didn't you and Carl take some time to see the sights when you came for the wedding or baptism?"

"Not really. We arrived on a Thursday and flew out on Monday both times."

"You came all this way and only stayed a few days?"

"I didn't really have a choice. It was a pretty busy time of year at work." I fail to also share that it was always a busy time of year at work. That's why I liked it. It validated me. Every day, I felt completely indispensable... until they dispensed of me, that is.

"What is it you do again?"

It says a lot about me that I'm surprised that he doesn't recall—as though I can't help feeling that my job is the only thing worth remembering about me. "I'm a lobbyist."

I brace myself for that usual look I get—sometimes coupled with a joke or two. Thanks to a few really bad eggs and a system that often turns a blind eye to corruption, people generally assume that I'm one of those evil lobbyists who puts our elected officials on the bankrolls of the special interests. Most of us aren't like that. Most of us are just trying to make politicians listen to the issues that people find important… which on some days should qualify us for sainthood.

Or at least a lesser version of it.

But instead of a joke or a look of disdain, he replies simply, "Well, you'll have some time to see Hawai'i on this trip, especially with Annie tied up till Baby K gets better. What is it you'd like to do while you're here?"

The question baffles me, which really says a lot about my vacationing prowess. "I—I really have no clue. I just pictured I'd be spending time with Annie and the baby. I thought maybe I could babysit a bit so that she and Cam could get a little time alone. I know that's hard to come by when you've got a baby."

"Oh, don't worry about them. They've got me here. And Fen flies in from O'ahu at least once a month for business."

"Fen got married last month, right?"

"Yeah. Beautiful ceremony on O'ahu."

"Annie texted me some photos." I smile at the image I draw up in my mind. I don't know Fen well at all—only spoke a few words to him at Annie's wedding and then a little at the baptism. But I'm grateful to Cam's brothers for being such a support to my friend in her new home.

I glance at Dodger. "Better watch out. All this marital bliss might be catching," I joke because seriously, with their flawless looks, he and Hailey looked like they belonged on the top of a wedding cake last time I saw them together.

"Mm. Yeah…" he grumbles.

I notice that his tone doesn't sound very enthusiastic. Maybe he's one of those devout single guys.

"Anyway," he continues, "Baby K's pretty spoiled by her uncles. She's our only niece, you know. So Cam and Annie get plenty of date nights. You like kids, then?"

"I hope Annie wouldn't have made me her baby's godmother if I didn't," I note almost boastfully because I really do like the title. I'd never admit it out loud, but I felt the tiniest hint of jealousy for Annie's friend Kaila when she was made the baby's namesake. So when I got to be godmother, I think my head swelled to three times its size right along with my heart. "Besides, I used to nanny a lot when I was getting my undergrad degree. That's kind of what Annie and I bonded over till—well, you know..." My voice trails, remembering Annie's last employer who caused her more than a headache, to say the least.

"Well, as crazy as all that was, I'm just glad that Annie ended up here. Because I wouldn't have a niece otherwise. Funny how the bad things sometimes bring the best things."

I nod briefly at his observation, hoping that the same will happen to me. Yet I'm unable to imagine that getting laid off will turn into anything but a pile of unpaid bills. If I hadn't had so many mileage points from all the travel I did for work, I never would have been daring enough to dip into my savings to come here right now. But I needed to get away, and won't have the time off for a while after I start a new job.

So here I am, smack dab in paradise without a clue what to do with my free time.

"I'll be headed to work after I get you settled in. I've got the evening shift," Dodger tells me. "You must be tired," he adds after a long span of silence between us makes my head start to tilt downward.

"Tired and hungry. Is there someplace close to where you live where I can pick up some food?"

"Very close. It's called my kitchen. But if you want something else, I live in a resort community. We've got a restaurant and bar right by our pool. A pretty good gym overlooking the water, too. In the winter, you can see whales breaching in the distance while you're running on the treadmill."

"Wow. That might inspire even me to work out. They don't have communities quite like that back home."

"Yeah. Most of the owners here rent out their homes to tourists. My brothers and I did that back when we were still in the Army."

"Sounds like heaven," I say as my eyes drift to the other-worldly landscape here on the Big Island. Hard, black lava is stretched out as far as I can see, pocked with tufts of tall grass. It's unsettling and yet awe-inspiring, just knowing that this land we're driving on was so newly created here on our planet. My trips for Annie's wedding and then for Kaila's baptism were both so rushed, I don't even recall taking in this view for more than a passing glance.

"Some people would call it that," he responds. "But I see where Cam lives now and can't help thinking it might be better for them. There are more playgroups for them up there—more friends for Baby K when she actually starts wanting playdates."

I eye him curiously. Words like *playgroups* and *playdates* sound different coming from a hot guy with biceps that bulge even when he's just holding a steering wheel.

Damn, it's sexy.

Lucky he's got a girlfriend or I'd be all over him like a politician on a stack of unregulated PAC money—a metaphor that's generally not appreciated outside of DC.

And hooking up on the rebound with my friend's brother-in-law has disaster written all over it.

CHAPTER 3

- DODGER -

It's been just long enough since my brothers moved out of our condo that I've become accustomed to coming home to an empty house each night.

It rarely bothers me. The novelty of sharing a house with my brothers wore off about three months after we'd all moved in together. I'd pull out my left kidney for either one of them without thinking twice. But what they did to the plumbing here is the kind of horror that only Stephen King would dare imagine.

So seeing a few lights on when I pull into my driveway just past midnight, I'm surprised that I feel a hint of satisfaction at the idea of having someone to come home to.

Samantha wasn't the most conversational woman on the ride back from the airport, struggling to string more than two sentences together after the overnight flight. And there was one point when I was pretty certain she was going to collapse.

But at least having her around will make the place less empty.

"You're up." My features, as tired as they are after a night of work, find the energy to offer a smile. Samantha's at my kitchen counter, looking deadly serious as she peers up at me from behind her open laptop. I glance at my watch, noting that where she hails from it must be time to wake up. "Jetlag?"

"I guess." She shuts her laptop as I approach. "I slept for a couple hours and then the silence woke me up."

"Not much silence where you are?"

"No. I'm in Capitol Hill in DC. It's pretty busy at all hours."

"Yeah, I imagine, especially if you're close to the Metro."

Her eyebrows rise. "You're familiar with the area?"

"Sure. I was stationed at the Pentagon once early in my career, and then my last post was at Walter Reed." I sit beside her. "You ever been to that pizza place near Eastern Market? Mario's Hot Pies?"

"You've been to Mario's?"

"Used to go there any chance I had. I've never found another place that made potato pizza."

Her upper lip curls. "I could never get myself to try that. Just didn't sound appetizing."

"No, no, you have to try it," I argue. "The potatoes are thinly sliced, almost like potato chips, spread over a pesto sauce. They were just a little firm and even had a bit of crunch to them. Then they'd top it off with radicchio and prosciutto. Damn..." My mind drifts. I know living in paradise has its benefits. But there are a lot of things I miss about the mainland. There were always new restaurants to try there. The Big Island is pretty undeveloped and when it comes to restaurants, what you see is what you get.

"Maybe I'll give it a try." Biting her bottom lip, she stands awkwardly and backs away from her laptop as though it's a temptation that is hard to resist. Then she glances at me as though I'm the distraction that she desperately needs. "So, Dr. Sheridan, how long does it take to get over jetlag?"

I give a light laugh. "It's different for everyone. The best thing to do is to try to get some sleep tonight and then force yourself to wake up at a normal hour. Just don't plan on doing too much tomorrow on so little sleep. Any plans?"

She sighs. "If Annie's still not up for company, I'll just be hanging out here, I guess. I've got some work I'll, uh, do online," she adds, looking strangely unsettled as she says it.

I tilt my head. "Aren't you on vacation?"

"Well, yeah. But there are some things I can get done from here."

I eye her, then her laptop, and then her again. It's like the damn thing has some kind of magnetic field that's pulling her in. "You know, as a doctor, I could go on and on about the benefits of taking time off from work."

Her lips form a tight line before she responds, "And as someone with bills to pay, I could go on and on about the benefits of being a workaholic. Besides, what else am I going to do at this hour?"

"Tons of things I like to do at night here. Go up the mountain to the telescopes they have out at Mauna Kea. Take a night snorkel tour to swim with the manta rays."

Cleary perplexed, she grimaces at my ideas. "Those sound a little ambitious for me."

"Okay, city girl. How about stargazing right here? That's easy enough." I stride across the room. "Come on."

"What?"

"Come on. Let's do it."

"I wasn't planning on—"

"You don't plan things on this island," I interrupt. "You just do them. Surf's up? Grab your board. Water's calm? Grab your snorkel gear. Volcano's active? Take a drive east. Got jetlag? Go stargaze." I grab my binoculars from the shelf. "You can probably see the Southern Cross at this hour," I add, seeing I still need to sell the idea.

"The what?"

"Southern Cross. The constellation. You won't see that in DC. So unless you're planning a trip to Australia…"

"Highly unlikely if I'm getting jetlag this bad from just being in Hawai'i," she interjects.

"…might as well, take advantage. Let's head to the beach."

"The beach? At this hour?"

I toss my chin in the direction of the water. "It's in my backyard. Come on."

She looks reluctant for a moment, glancing down at her laptop again. I can't imagine what work she's got waiting for her that could possibly edge its way into a Hawai'i vacation. Yet I remember that feeling—that need to be so attached to my work and that addictive validation I'd feel every time my phone rang after-hours.

But apparently, the lure of stars is enough to get her to follow me.

Grabbing a couple beach towels from the mudroom, I go in bare feet. It's just steps from my door and I like the feel of the sand between my toes. We slip through an opening in the hedge and just like that, the worries of my day fall away. It's like that with the ocean and me—something about the smell of the salt air and the sound of the surf erases the monotony of the colds and jellyfish stings and stomach bugs that I deal with at the urgent care center every day. Dealing with tourists at a doc-in-box is a little like fixing people up as they pass on a conveyor belt. They come, they go, they generally leave a good review online, and I never see them again. I can't say I like it much.

But then I feel the presence of this ocean and it all washes away. Just above the water, I see the stars that form the Southern Cross. I glance in Samantha's direction as we stop along the shoreline. "There it is. Low in the sky there."

"There what is?"

"The Southern Cross."

"Neat," she says dismissively. "Very cool. Really. Thanks. But I should probably get back to what I was doing on my laptop."

"You're a textbook workaholic, aren't you?" I chuckle.

There's just enough light from the stars that I can see her eyes narrow. "You know, back home, that's a compliment," she informs me. "We glorify workaholics. But here, I think you're trying to insult me."

"Not insult you, especially seeing as I used to be one myself. I'm just trying to get you to slow down and take time to smell the saltwater." I stretch the towels on the sand and lie down on one.

The hint of a frown forms on her lips. "I really don't need to lie down. I can see them just fine from up here."

"I *dare* you."

"What?"

"I dare you to just lie down here and completely relax."

Looking strangely threatened by the idea, she laughs warily. "I don't relax."

"Well, then I win," I say in the most childish tone I can muster.

She cocks her head. "I thought you were supposed to be the *mature* Sheridan brother."

"I am. That doesn't say much for my brothers, does it?"

She glances around as though just lying in the sand is something she wouldn't be caught dead doing back on the mainland. "Okay, fine." She joins me on the towel next to me. "Happy?"

"*You* will be in a minute."

"I get it, okay? The stars are gorgeous." She says it like she's just trying to appease me. "Seriously. So much better than any I see back home."

"Just wait."

"For what?"

"Your eyes to adjust." We lay there in blessed silence for a while; I'm grateful for it because I feel like every word that comes out of her mouth hints of an argument.

"Oh my..." She breathes out suddenly just at a point when I was wondering if she dozed off.

I grin at the sight of the Milky Way above us. "That's your home galaxy. Pretty damn amazing, isn't?"

"My God. I've never see it so clear."

"You didn't see this when you visited?" I ask, even though I suspected that was the case.

"No. I guess I never took the time to look up. It was always pretty much go-go-go from the moment we arrived here."

I pull my binoculars out of their case. "Okay, so I'm going to blow you away even more. See Orion's belt over here? Those three stars right there." I point.

"Yeah."

"Now see those couple stars just below that third one?" I peek through the binos just to confirm I've got it right. Then I see it, and I smile this time, just like all the others because it never gets old. I hand the binoculars to her. "Take a look at them through these. Be sure to press the image stabilization button on the top," I finish as she holds them up to her eyes.

"This one?"

"No. That's the focus. This one on top." Rolling over to

my side, I reach for her hand and guide her finger to the button.

I'm stunned by the rush I feel when our skin touches.

But I shrug it off. Between the sound of the waves crashing and the starlight above us, it's no wonder I'd feel what some might call a "spark" in this moment.

"This one?"

Her breath seems to catch as she asks me, and I wonder if she felt that same sensation that I did. "Yes, that one," I tell her. "And look right there."

She lifts her eyes from the binos once more to get her bearings and then peers through them again.

"Yep. Just there where that little cluster is." I watch her as she searches and know the instant she sees it.

"Oh my God. What is that?"

"That is the Orion Nebula."

"Seriously? I never knew you could see such a thing with binoculars."

My smile widens. I've forgotten what it's like to share something completely new with someone. I can practically feel her excitement in the air around her.

I never got that sense when I'd do things with Hailey. She was a geologist here on the Big Island for a two-year stint with the National Park Service, and is an avid adventurer—hiker, diver, snorkeler, kite boarder, skydiver. When I met her, she'd already been on-island for a while and had experienced a lot of what we have here. Which is probably why she bolted the moment she got a new job with the Service at the Grand Canyon. It was time for her to move on.

So it's refreshing to see the surprise on Samantha's face when she experiences something new. And I'll admit, it makes something surge inside of me that shouldn't—this desire to show her so much more that Hawai'i has to offer her. As I look at her now, I remember my own excitement when I first settled into the rhythm of this island and opened my eyes to paradise.

"Oh, that's nothing." I sit up now, looking closer to the horizon. "Can I see those again?" She hands me the binos and I find what I'm looking for. "Okay, so... see that star right there?" I point. "Look at that through the binos and then just start to slowly move downward toward the horizon. When you see a blur—kind of like a thumbprint in the sky, you're there."

She takes the binos from me and follows my directions. "I see it. Is that another nebula?"

"Nope. That's the Andromeda galaxy."

"You're kidding me!"

"No. That's it. One trillion stars right there in that little smudge in the sky. Two-and-a-half million light years from us. So all that light you're seeing right now took two-and-a-half million years to even reach your eyes."

Her sigh is like a low, appreciative whistle. "Two-and-a-half million years. It's like looking into the past. That's just hard to even fathom."

"I know," I agree, liking how much her tone has changed since she got on the beach. It's dark, but there's just enough starlight that I can see her smile with amazement, as though I just revealed to her the innermost workings of the universe, and now she's free to discover her own place in it.

"It makes me feel so insignificant—and yet so significant at the same time, you know?" She barely whispers it, words laced with awe, before she scoffs, "That doesn't even make sense, though."

"Makes sense to me," I tell her with a hint of admiration because it took a couple years on this island for me to figure that out. Maybe she's grasped it a little more quickly than I did. I lift my eyebrows. "Makes you want to make every day count, doesn't it?"

"Yeah," she says, her eyes still glued to my binos.

"Like putting away your laptop and cell phone and maybe having a real vacation," I can't resist suggesting.

Her eyes peer over the top of the binos at me. "You totally set me up for that one." She sighs. "But you're right. Truth is, I just don't know what people *do* on vacations. I travel all the time for work, but not for fun. Last time I took days off, it was for a bout of pneumonia."

I tuck in my chin. "I think we can do better than that."

"We?"

"Sure. No offense, but you need serious help in the vacation department. My life *is* a vacation since I moved here." I say it as though it's something to be proud of. Yet when I look at her and see the stranglehold her career seems to have on her, there's this strange part of me that envies that. Since coming to the island, my life revolves around play the same way hers does around work. I can't help missing the sense of dedication to my career that I had before I came here. "I can show you around the island."

"You really don't have to do that. Besides, there are things I really should do while I'm here."

Eyeing her, I can sense her conjuring up the image of her laptop right now. I've been there. I get it.

"So do them while I'm at work," I compromise. I tilt my head at her, watching her clutch the binoculars as though she's just not ready to give them up. "You can't tell me you're regretting coming out here tonight."

She lowers the binos to her chest and just gazes at the expanse of the universe above us. "No. No regrets."

"So we'll get out and see some of the island before I go in for my evening shift tomorrow. If you hate it, you can spend the rest of your time here staring at your laptop and I won't say a word about it."

"Not a word?"

"Scout's honor," I tell her.

"Okay," she sighs. "Tomorrow, I'm yours."

I'm yours. I have no idea why those two words are having a primal effect on me. Blame the stars or the waves or the sand between my toes. But it definitely confirms...

I'm no scout.

CHAPTER 4

~ SAMANTHA ~

Who turned on my white noise app?

That's my first thought as I awaken to near silence—except for the sound of waves crashing against the shore. With my eyes still shut, I can only imagine I must have turned on my white noise app last night to drown out the traffic or the sound of my neighbors watching reruns of *Live PD.*

It only takes a moment for me to remember where I am. It's hard to forget because my body is melded to this memory foam mattress and, in my mind's eye, I can still see the stars above me right now.

I'm in Hawai'i.

I'm in Hawai'i, and I have zero interest in checking to see if any texts or emails came in last night.

Wow.

Wow. This feels really good.

Until it doesn't anymore. Because, just as I would predict, my brain starts clicking and I feel the urge to roll over and grab my phone. Since I got laid off, I've been struck every morning by how empty my life feels without work greeting my day with a barrage of texts and emails.

I've felt that ache each time I'd reach for my phone at daybreak and realize that I have nowhere that I need to be, not a single meeting or conference call scheduled, and not even one calendar reminder to make me feel like I have some kind of value.

Even after seven interviews these past three weeks, I'm still without a job offer.

I should just lie here for a while, try this "relax" concept that Dodger was trying to sell me last night. I'm almost tempted to just leave my phone off for the day. I kind of made a promise, and as they say, a watched pot never boils. But then I remember Annie and her baby and want to see if she's texted me with an update.

I hope little Kaila is all better. For her. For Annie. And just a little bit for me so that I can have some purpose for my trip again. Because I'm a person who needs a purpose. So as I instinctively reach for my phone, I open my eyes.

Another sunny day on the Kona side of the island.

I can remember Annie texting me these words so many times since she moved here. And each time, I'd stare at the unpredictable skies of Washington, DC, and think she must be exaggerating.

Maybe she's not.

Maybe the days really are always sunny here.

And maybe all men here are like Dodger Sheridan. Maybe every damn one of them has a warm smile to greet weary women at the airport and strong arms for dragging unwieldy luggage. Maybe they all so patiently coax workaholics out onto the beach for a night of stargazing.

Maybe. But probably not. My cheeks puff out and I release a slow, appreciative sigh.

No. I think that's just Dodger.

Hailey is the luckiest woman on the face of the earth.

I used to say that about Annie because she had Cam. But now that she's shared with me every gory detail of pregnancy and childbirth, I can't help thinking her lucky score has dropped just a point or two.

There's a text from my mom awaiting me. I give it a quick glance. "U should buy something for the people in your office while u r there. Let them know u appreciate the week off," she writes.

I frown. I know Mom means well, but I don't know why every text she sends me always has to do with my job.

My job that I no longer have. I reply with a quick thumbs-up emoji and then open the text that Annie sent me.

"Did u sleep all right?" it reads.

"Best sleep in ages," I write back and am surprised when I immediately see the little dots that tell me she's replying.

"Wish I could say the same."

Worry wrinkles my brow. "Is K any better?" I tap in.

"A little. But I'm coming down with it now, I think."

"O no!"

"O yes. Dodger stopped by this morn. Got me something for this cough that kept me up. Already feeling a lot better. So tired tho."

"How about I come over and take care of K so u can recover?" I offer, liking the idea of being needed.

"No. Cam's taking care of both of us now. U just stay away and stay healthy. Is Dodger taking good care of u?"

A smile threatens—the kind of smile that reeks of adolescent crush. I give myself a shake. I really must be on the rebound, because I usually don't respond this way to men with girlfriends. I believe in Girl Code, all the way.

"Yep," I reply simply, scared that if I used any more words than that, my friend would read my mind.

My dirty, dirty mind.

"Good. Try 2 have some fun while u r here. I just feel sick about this."

There's a pause before my phone chimes again as she adds, "Literally," along with a smiley face emoji.

"Don't. Just get better," I tap in. "I'm not leaving till I get 2 see that beautiful goddaughter of mine!"

"You just gave me incentive to stay sick. I'd love it if u stayed forever."

I smile, thinking how impossible that is for a person like me. "LOL. Not many lobbyists here. Besides, I break out in a rash if I relax 2 much." Or if I relax at all, I want to add but don't.

"Well, at least u r staying with a doc!"

Now, why'd she have to write that? The last thing I need is to start fantasizing about playing doctor with Dodger.

"Go back 2 bed," I type in. "Text if u need anything. I'm immune 2 the worst the world has 2 offer. I work with politicians, remember?"

She sends me a thumbs-up emoji and I switch over to email just to make sure that one didn't slip in without sending me an alert.

Nothing. I stare at my phone for a moment, refreshing the display with the hope that I'll see an email appear with a job offer. Then I stare some more, the same way I sometimes look into the refrigerator for something good to eat even though I know there's nothing tasty in there.

Emptiness swells inside me. I hate this. I hate being unemployed. I hate that I wasted so many years of my life at a firm that cast me off like a pariah when times weren't perfect anymore.

Kind of the same way Carl did.

Pressing my lips together at the thought, it's hard not to let the tears fall right now, the way they often do at this time of day.

But I'm rescued by a knock at the bedroom door as I set down my phone.

"Yes?" I say, quickly remembering that I've only got a nightshirt on, and hoping that Dodger won't burst in.

And in the next instant, I'm hoping he will.

"I heard your phone, so I knew you were up," he tells me through the door.

"Caught," I confess. "But I'm just texting Annie," I quickly add, remembering I had told him I'd steer away from work today, which should be easy seeing as I'm jobless, I suppose.

"Yeah, I just came from their place. I brought home some avocado toast from a coffeehouse up the road. It's a favorite on the island. Annie said you'd love it."

My eyes light. This man was plucked from my best fantasies. A guy who can look like a Greek God who brings me avocado toast?

This *is* paradise. And I'd wager it has nothing to do with Hawai'i and everything to do with *him* until I throw on some clothes, go downstairs, and see the epicurean delight he has waiting for me in a takeout box.

"Oh my God." It's not toast he's brought me. It's a masterpiece. "I've never seen avocados this ripe in my life."

He's making coffee in the Keurig and I'm plunging deeper into this fantasy I seem to be in as he hands me a mug when it's filled... until he shatters it all by saying, "Yeah. Hailey loved that place." He juts his chin in the direction of the take-out container.

Yep, that was just enough to bring me back to reality. "But not anymore?"

He gives his head a shake. "She developed an avocado allergy."

I glance down at the toast and feel a rush of pity for this woman. Even though she *does* look like a paddle-boarding-yoga-goddess, no one should be deprived of this. "That's horrible."

He chuckles. "It's just an allergy. Not the end of the world."

"I suppose," I say, then taking my first bite. My lashes flutter downward and I expel a low moan as I chew. "I take that back. If you told me I couldn't have this again, it *would* be the end of the world." I glance at what he's eating, a bowl brimming with a design of sliced fruits I don't even recognize. "What's that?"

"Hawaiian acai bowl," he replies, his words muffled with food in his mouth. "Want some?"

I shake my head, then cock it to the side, reconsidering. "Maybe a bite. Would you mind?"

He scoops out a heaping spoonful saturated with every color in the rainbow. As he holds it out to me, I lean in and let my lips wrap around the spoon while it's still in his grasp.

Realizing suddenly that he probably was expecting me to *take* the spoon—not lick it clean while he's holding it like I'm trying to seduce him—I flush with embarrassment.

"Sorry," I say, grabbing it out of his hand to finish the bite. "I get a little over-enthusiastic at the sight of fresh fruit like this. Is it my imagination, or does everything taste better on Hawai'i?"

He laughs. "You wouldn't say that if you tasted the milk they bring in from the mainland. You'd find out why I always spring for the local stuff. The cows have more aloha."

I feel my smile widen, and the sensation of it takes a fast path straight to my heart. I don't know why exactly, but when I talk to him, I seem to feed off of his easy mannerisms and casual humor. For a guy in a Type A kind of job, he has this inner calm that I envy.

I want to be more like him. I want to be able to easily list ten things I'd like to do with some free time.

My list is limited to one now that I don't have work in my life: Sleep. I freakin' love sleep.

"So, what time do you go to work today? Is it always in the evenings?" I ask.

"It varies as much as I want it to. I don't like to fall into a rut."

"Most people like predictability," I can't help pointing out, somehow missing the predictability of a paycheck right now.

"Not me. If I worked the evening shift every day, I'd miss too many sunsets. If I worked the morning shift, I'd miss our sunrises."

"How about the midday shift?"

"Ah, then I'd miss what I'm going to do with you today."

I lift a single hand, remembering our deal from last night. "Look, I said I'd lay off my computer today, and I will. But you've got better things to do than to play cruise director to my life while I'm here."

"I was just going to check on Baby K and Annie before I headed into work tonight. But other than that, I'm free. We could hang out at Mauna Kea Beach right here. Catch some rays. Maybe I could show you how to boogie board. Or we could go to the volcano. I checked the NPS website and there's some pretty good lava flow today."

My ears perk up. "Lava flow? I'm in."

He looks surprised. "Really?"

"Yeah. I kind of wished I had taken the time to see it when I came out for the wedding."

"I'd have pegged you more as the lie on the beach with a margarita type."

"I'm full of surprises," I tell him, somehow unable to admit that lying on a beach without my phone or laptop sounds like my version of hell.

43

"I'm discovering that. I'll call Hailey and see if she can get a park ranger to point us in the right direction of the flow when we get there. She'll probably know someone who's working at the visitor center today."

"That's right. She's a geologist, isn't she?"

"Yeah. How quickly can you get ready? It's a bit of a haul to get there."

I shrug. "I can be ready in fifteen minutes."

"Girl after my own heart."

I escape upstairs to put on some makeup, hoping I made it out of the kitchen before he saw me blush at his words. Girl after his heart? A dangerous thing for a man with a girl-friend to say to a woman on the rebound, even if he was joking.

Lucky for him, I have some scruples.

Though in his presence, I'm discovering they are in limited supply.

CHAPTER 5

- DODGER -

I've spent a lot of time with Hailey on this volcano, so I should know it like the back of my hand. But the amazing thing about the landscape at Volcanoes National Park is that it's always changing. So I'm glad that my text to Hailey this morning resulted in a park ranger meeting us at the entrance with a hand-notated map of where the lava flow is today.

That says a lot about the way she and I broke things off. It was amicable—almost logical in nature, the same way our relationship tended to be.

I should miss her; I can't help thinking that sometimes. But after those first couple weeks after she left, the only time I really miss her is when I'm out on a painfully bad date, usually with someone who can name all the Kardashians but can't tell me the name of the Vice President.

I remember visiting Fen on O'ahu before he got married

to Kaila. She traveled a lot for work back then, and I couldn't help noticing a change in his personality when she was gone.

"There's a piece of me missing when I'm away from her," he had explained to me when I'd asked, probably the most sentimental statement I've ever heard from him.

I didn't give it a second thought back then. But now, I can't help envying my brother for that connection—likely the same way Cam feels about Annie.

Because here I am, not missing Hailey that way, even after a year of dating her.

Except for the sex. I miss the sex.

"So how is Carl doing these days?" I ask Samantha at that thought, feeling the need to remind myself that the guy exists.

She seems flustered. "Fine," she replies, quickly tacking on, "Wouldn't see him out here on a volcano, though. Hey—what's that over there?"

The way she whipped that conversation around reminds me of some of the little kids who end up in my examining room. *"I've got sniffles. Look at my purple bruise! Did they have Barney when you were little?"*

My gaze follows to where she's pointing. "More lava?" I answer more like a question.

"I mean, it looks different from what we're walking on."

"That's *'a'a*. It's the jagged kind. What we're walking on is *pahoehoe*. It's smoother—better for hiking on after it cools and hardens, definitely. I get a few tourists in my clinic every week who trip on *'a'a* and need stitches."

"Impressive. Did Hailey teach you that?"

"Actually, I knew that before I met her. Living here, you learn a lot of things that you never thought you'd know."

"Like what else?"

"Well, you learn about lava zones and tsunami zones as soon as you start looking at real estate."

"Don't tell me about any of that until after I leave, okay?"

"I'll make a note of that. And you learn a lot about the stars," I add.

"I can understand that after last night."

"If you liked that, I could take you up to Mauna Kea. They've got telescopes at the visitors' center they'll let you use. Makes those binos we used last night look like a toy prize you'd win at Chuck E. Cheese. It's pretty amazing."

She glances behind her to where we were. "I just saw lava pouring out of the bowels of the earth," she says with noted dramatic flair. "That's going to be hard to beat."

"Yeah, we got lucky. The volcano's been pretty unpredictable lately."

"Unpredictable." She tucks in her chin. "I'd have preferred you said that *after* we were safely on the other side of the island again."

I chuckle. "Don't feel too safe there. That airport you flew into was built on the 1801 lava flow of Hualalai, just one of our five volcanoes on this island."

"But it's dormant now, right?"

"Nope. Active."

"Wait—what?"

"Yeah. Some people say it's expected to erupt again sometime in the next hundred years."

Her face screws up in horror.

"Hey," I assure her, "a hundred years is a long time."

"Not long enough."

"You take a much bigger risk driving in that DC traffic than I do living on a volcano," I counter.

"True," she says thoughtfully. "But it can't be good for your property value if that thing starts rumbling," she replies.

Somehow it's just the type of statement I'd expect from her.

"Maybe," I agree. "But our views are worth it."

She sends me a conciliatory nod. "Nature's got the upper hand here. But you can't deny that when it comes to things that are manmade, DC really has something to offer."

"Like?" I egg her on, even though, having lived there, I don't need to be reminded. I guess I just enjoy the way she talks so passionately about things that once meant something to me.

"Our monuments. Our architecture. Our museums."

"Your restaurants," I toss in. "I'm so damn tired of hearing the words, 'Our special today is mahi-mahi.'"

She laughs, and it strikes me how much I enjoy the sound of it. It makes my heart pinch in an unfamiliar way that I'd really like to blame on the Spam musabi I ate for lunch, a Hawaiian favorite.

But it's not the musabi. It's her.

"Yeah, and you don't have crab cakes like we do," she reminds me.

Feigning heart failure, I grab my chest. "You're killing me, lady. I love crab cakes." My mouth actually salivates as I say it.

"So you gave up the best crab cakes on the planet to live on an active volcano," she retorts, her tone mocking me.

"Oh, come on. Look around you." I spread my arms out. "This place is addictive. You can't deny that."

"I won't. But I'll remind you of that if this whole place blows like Krakatoa."

"It's a shield volcano," I point out. "So it's not usually as violent."

"*Usually.*" She chuckles under her breath. "That's one of those words you never like to hear in the same sentence as *volcano.*"

Enjoying this conversation with her way too much, I grin. I like the way, no matter what I say, she quickly volleys the ball right back to me. There's a certain energy when we talk, and yet it never seems forced.

I picture her boyfriend—how disinterested he seemed in the world outside of his phone, and I can't imagine her talking to him like this. Why is she wasting her time with someone like that?

Not that it's any of my business.

I give myself an internal shrug before noting, "For someone who worries so much about volcanoes, you sure jumped at the chance to see one up close."

She shoots me a smile. "I work with politicians. I crave volatility."

"And you love it," I notice as her eyes brighten.

"I do." Her grin widens. Then it falters for a moment as if she remembered something about work that she left hanging to come here. Then it returns as she adds, "I mean, I don't really like politicians in general. But most of them aren't as bad as that idiot Annie worked for." She pauses, then amends, "*Most*. But I love feeling like my work actually means something. I mean, you're a doctor. You get that feeling all the time, I'm sure."

You get that feeling all the time, I'm sure. I feel a frown pinch the sides of my mouth as her words ring in my mind—reminding me of something I hate to admit. It's been years since I felt that sense of purpose I used to crave. Contrary to what she's saying, the biggest difference I generally make at my urgent care clinic is advising patients that, no, you really *aren't* supposed to pee on a jellyfish sting.

Which pales in comparison to what I used to do.

I see the enthusiasm in her eyes as she talks about work, and I remember when I had that spark inside me—a handful of years and forty-five hundred miles ago.

When I was in the Army, I knew I could do my job better

than anyone else. I knew that at the end of the day, Soldiers were better off because I was there for them.

I was damn good at what I did.

Ironically, that's why I had to leave.

Damn bureaucracy.

"So what is it you love about lobbying?" I ask, not wanting this track of conversation to end.

"Well, I don't love the bad reputation we all seem to have," she laughs. "And don't get me wrong—we have our share of shady characters. I mean, seriously..." She shakes her head as her voice trails for a moment. "But when I convince some senators to vote for a bill—that can mean things like more funding for research on a disease or more protections for the environment or better healthcare or more jobs. Things that really *mean* something to people. It feels good—to think that I'm doing something that changes lives."

Annoyance prickles through me when her phone rings. I can't help it. It's as though I'm reluctant to share her.

When she retrieves it from her back pocket, I glance over at her. She looks excited and expectant at the same time, like she's been waiting for an important call.

But when she sees the name that appears, the spark in her eyes fizzles.

"Hey, Mom," she answers.

As she talks, I can't help wondering why she seemed so hopeful when her phone first rang. To me, technology is a bit of a nuisance.

"No, I know," she's saying, her voice strained. "I saw that text and I replied already. It's a great idea. But—" She takes a lengthy pause, listening. "I'm on vacation. I don't need to check in with work... Mom, I'm sorry. I don't mean to cut you off, but Dodger and I are on a hike... Cam's brother.... Right... uh-huh. Well, I did come here to see the baby, but she's sick right now..."

I nearly laugh at Samantha's lavish eye roll.

"I didn't *know* she was sick when I left. Seriously, Mom, can I text you later? I'm in the middle of a lava field and... No, I'm serious... Yes, I'm being careful... Okay. Love you, too." She lets out a pained sigh after she hangs up. "Sorry. That was rude of me. I should have let that go to voicemail."

"It's no problem." I glance over, hoping the light will return to her eyes because I love to see it there.

"She's not normally so intrusive. Seriously. But every time I tell her I'm taking any time off work, she turns into this other woman, I swear it."

"Does she get uneasy when you travel or something?" As an Army doc, I saw plenty of people with anxiety and the damnedest things can trigger it.

"No. She just hates it when I take off work. Always thinks I'll get fired for it," she says uneasily. "I'm thirty years old, and she still acts like I'm working at my first job at the fro yo place near my school."

"Parents never like to think that we've grown up."

"That's probably true." Her laugh is half-hearted until her face turns somber. "Sometimes *I* kind of wish I wasn't grown up, too."

I literally cringe at the idea. "Not me."

"Really?"

"Hell no. All that teenage angst? And the pimples. God, don't forget those."

Her face elongates as she looks at me. "I'm trying to picture you as a pimple-pocked teen, Dodger, and I just can't do it."

"I was. And gangly. All us Sheridan kids were when we were younger. Even my cousins."

"Well, you certainly came into your own." She gives me a smile that's almost flirtatious, which I can't help returning in kind.

"You, too," I say simply, even though there's this part of me that wants to elaborate—to tell her that right now, with her hair pulled back haphazardly and her skin flushed from a fairly ambitious hike, she looks like my version of perfection in a woman, and I can't even quite pinpoint why.

It's as though my eyes were somehow programmed to easily rest on her face and find calm in the sight of it.

But I doubt Carl would appreciate that sentiment.

"Tell me more about what you do," I say instead, anxious again to see that excitement in her eyes as she talks about work, especially as we get in my Jeep and head back so that I can spend another evening fixing up patients whom I'll never see again.

So I listen to her, feeding off her excitement as we make our way back home.

CHAPTER 6

~ SAMANTHA ~

For the record, I'm a fraud.

I love helping people with their problems, but struggle to share my own.

It's never held me back. In fact, quite the opposite. I learned at an early age that people generally don't want to know about my problems; they just want an answer to theirs.

Yet I still feel like a fraud when I'm with Dodger. There's something between us that makes me just want to confide in him—as though I should tell him that I've lost my job... that my boyfriend dumped me... that those business cards that once defined me are no longer in my purse.

And that I *really* should get myself to a hotel because I'm hopelessly, undeniably attracted to him.

He's got the kind of arms that would feel so good just wrapped around me as I pour out my heart. I could picture it —and even dare to—me, snuggled into him as he holds me close, my head resting against his chest so that I can hear his heartbeat as I cry it out.

Just *cry it out* like I always hear people should do from time to time.

Just cry it out like I am right now, nestled into a way-too-comfy bed, muffling my sobs with a duvet and staring at a cell phone that only seems to bring me rejection emails like the one I'm looking at right now:

"Thank you for taking the time to meet with us last week. Unfortunately, the position has been filled."

I stare at the words on my phone's display and let the tears fall.

Normally, it would be my mother's shoulder I'd cry on in the worst of times. We've always been close that way. So when a bully at school called me a name or a pack of girls in college wouldn't accept me into their crowd, I could always rely on a listening ear from Mom.

And when a boy broke my heart, I'd have not just her shoulder, but the reassurance that if a boy had the power to break my heart, I was better off without him anyway, because happiness is more secure when a man isn't wrapped up in the package.

Mom is good that way, saying the things I need to hear and giving me a handful of her courage at a time when I need it the most.

But I can't call her about this. And if I can't tell her about my job, then I can't tell her about Carl either, since one story pretty much requires the other.

The loss of a job wouldn't bring me a hefty dose of coddling. Instead, it would likely bring me a kick-in-the-ass lecture that I better get out there and dredge up another employer—even though that's what I've been trying to do for three weeks now.

DC is one of those places where one minute you're the

freshest stick of gum in the pack, and the next minute, you're being scraped off someone's shoe. I've seen it happen to others.

But even when I was laid off, I refused to believe it was happening to me. It was just a minor setback, I had pondered then. It was an opportunity for me to find something better at a time when I'd thought I was at the height of my career and would be snatched up by another employer.

Apparently, I was wrong.

I wipe my eyes with the sheet and put my phone back on the nightstand. Picking up the remote, I move my adjustable bed into the sitting position—not because I want it that way, but just because I can. I swear as soon as I get a job, I'm buying a bed like this.

Because I will get a job. I have to.

Outside, I can hear the ocean; I'm just savvy enough about island life now to know that if I sleep with my window open, I can be awakened by the salt-scented breeze and the crashing of the waves. How I'll ever go back to street noise outside my window is beyond me.

When I rally myself to head downstairs, I'm actually relieved to not see Dodger in the kitchen. Resisting him is a little much to ask of a girl before coffee, especially when I'm feeling the need for a shoulder to cry on.

And what shoulders he's got.

"Morning," he greets me as he comes in from the lanai holding an empty cereal bowl. "How'd you sleep last night?"

Damn. There he is, looking even more tempting before my morning surge of caffeine.

"Great," I force myself to reply. "I think that hike on the volcano helped my jetlag, even though I did wake up at midnight feeling like I should be eating dinner." I fumble with his Keurig until he slides up to me and takes over. In truth, I still have the old-fashioned kind of coffeemaker. My mom bought me one when I got my first apartment and I'm just sentimental enough to not want to let it go.

"I hope I didn't wake you. I usually roll in around then," he says.

"Yet you still get up early?"

"I got enough sleep." He pours himself a glass of passion fruit juice from his fridge. His eyes narrow as he looks at me. "You all right? Your eyes look a little red."

My back straightens and I turn away to retrieve the creamer. "I'm fine. My eyes are just a little irritated. Probably that—what was it you called it at the volcano yesterday? That haziness from the volcano's gases?"

"Vog. Yeah, that can get to you sometimes. There are eye drops we can pick up for it, if you want."

"Nah, I'll be fine." I'll be fine if I can just avoid tears for a while, I add in my head.

"Come join me on the lanai, if you'd like."

I've still got my back to him, but when the quiet tells me that he's left the kitchen, I slump my shoulders and expel a long breath.

If I was smart, I'd stir some creamer in my coffee and head straight back upstairs. But Dodger Sheridan is like a box of matches and I'm five years old again. I know it's not smart to play with fire, but I'm gonna do it anyway.

Besides, the surge of hormones I experience around him might do wonders to dispel the gloom of unemployment.

Outside, the ocean is so vibrant that it almost hurts my eyes. I soak in the sight of it for a moment before speaking. "I'd like to do something to thank Hailey for yesterday. She really got us hooked up. I mean, I'll never see something like that again in my life."

He waves a hand. "Don't worry about it. She loves sharing the Parks like that, making sure people have a good time.

Kind of goes with the career. And considering you can't deny you had fun yesterday—"

"I wouldn't even *try* to deny that," I interject.

"—I thought maybe I'd convince you to go snorkeling today. I've got a friend who leads catamaran tours and he kind of owes me since I stitched up his girlfriend's shark bite a couple weeks ago. There were a couple last-minute cancellations, so he offered the spots to me."

I should be wondering why he'd invite me rather than Hailey, but I'm trying to wrap my head around something else entirely. "Did you really just invite me snorkeling in the same breath that you said the words *shark bite?*"

He grins. "Come on. Nothing in that water is nearly as dangerous as those politicians you face in DC."

"I'd argue that point."

"Should be fun. The tour goes out to Kealakekua Bay. It's the best way to see the Captain Cook monument."

"A monument?"

"Yeah. It marks where he was killed by the native Hawaiians."

My brow scrunches. "Why does everything that comes out of your mouth this morning scare me?"

He cocks his head. "Come on. Everyone else I know is working today. Do I have to dare you again?"

"Believe me, it will take more than a dare to get me to play the role of shark bait for the morning."

His gaze intensifies. "Samantha, I swear I won't let anything happen to you. Besides the fact that it goes against the Hippocratic Oath, my sister-in-law would kill me."

Even with his joking tone as he says it, I can't deny the warmth that cascades over me. Something about him makes me feel... protected. A guy like him wouldn't desert a girl if a shark was making a beeline toward her.

For that matter, a guy like him wouldn't dump a girl when she lost her job.

If I was Hailey, I'd be taking the day off work just to have more of this sensation.

But since she's working... well, someone might as well enjoy it.

"Okay. Thanks." I pause and nibble on my lower lip for a moment before I add, "I think."

There's a fluttering in my belly at the thought of spending another day with Dodger—no matter how I try to suppress it. It seems to nudge out those feelings of self-doubt and failure that consumed me as I stared at yet another rejection email this morning. I've always been practical about men, and never indulged in temptation on the scale that Dodger seems to provide. My mom taught me early on that love, lust, and all its horny derivations should be based on shared mutual goals in life, not something as flighty as hormones.

But tell that to the butterflies in my stomach.

CHAPTER 7

- DODGER -

I really need to get laid.

I realize it the moment I hold open the door to my Jeep and get an eyeful of leg as Samantha hoists herself into the passenger seat.

I've had this car for a year or two, and the oversized wheels help when I off-road on my way to Waipi'o Valley.

But today I'm noting this secondary benefit.

When a woman is off-market, I tend to not feel attraction. I'm not blind; it's not that I wouldn't *notice* that Samantha has really gorgeous, muscular legs—probably from walking all over DC. Or that her eyes are the most curious color, convincing me in some lighting that they are as blue as the ocean, but in the next minute, they look like they're green. And then there's those lips.

Don't get me started about those lips.

But when a woman is spoken for, those tend to be more

like scientific observations. They don't soak past the surface and get into my bloodstream, tempting my brain into some delicious fantasies.

Still, I can't help noting that Carl is 4,500 miles away right now. And it strikes me as odd that *not once* in the two days she's been staying with me have I seen them talking on the phone together.

He probably just texts her. It seems more his style.

I get in beside her and head south toward a marina near downtown Kona where we'll meet the boat. It's about a half hour drive, and yet I find the air between us is always filled with conversation—about DC, about careers, about things she'd like to see while she's here. And in the few instances when there is a lull, there's nothing awkward about it. For some reason, I seem to enjoy simply being near her.

"Oh, wow—a coffee farm?" she blurts out suddenly when she sees a sign near the road.

"Yeah. They do tours, too. Interested?"

"Absolutely. Coffee is considered sacred in DC, you know. Will we have time today after the boat?"

I shake my head. "I'll need to head into work. But it's a straight shot down here if you want to go on your own."

"Oh, I'll wait and go with you. I mean… just if you want."

Oh, I want, I ponder silently. *I want too much with you.* "Sure. We can make a day of it." I pause a moment and, trying to keep myself in check, I add, "If Baby K and Annie are better, they can come along."

And while I want them to feel better, there's this wicked side of me that can't resist wanting to keep Samantha to myself. "If you like those types of tours, I know there's a vanilla farm tour nearby, too."

"Sounds great. Back home I always hear about tours like that—organic farms and wineries and apiaries outside the beltway. Like in Loudon County or the Shenandoah. But I never find the time to actually go."

I glance over at her silence as she looks thoughtful for a moment.

"I think I need to rectify that." She says it quietly, as though it's more to herself than to me.

"No one ever said on their deathbed that they wished they spent more time at work," I say, something my brothers used to tell me when I lived in DC.

"You know, I never really minded until now," she considers. "The long nights and working weekends. Because I really do love what I do. But I think now that I'm here—kind of on the outside looking in at my life—I see how unhealthy it was."

"Did you always want to be a lobbyist?"

"No. I never gave the career a second thought until I saw the ad for the job. It was an entry-level position I started at."

"What did you want to be?"

"You mean, like, growing up?"

"Yeah."

"Employed," she laughs. "Seriously, that's all I ever really wanted. My mom used to drill that into me when I was a kid. 'Don't be like me,' she'd say. 'You get your degree. Find something where you don't have to work for minimum wage.'"

She does a pretty funny imitation of her mother's voice as she says it.

"I have to agree with her there," I reply. "And the minimum wage jobs are usually the hardest ones out there. When I was in high school, I worked at a donut shop in our hometown and it nearly broke me. To this day, I've never seen a busier rush hour than at Pop's Donuts on a Saturday morning."

"I've always thought it should be a requirement for people to work one of those types of jobs," she says in that logical tone a logical guy like me can't help appreciating. "I don't care who you are or how much money you have," she continues. "Nothing at Yale or Harvard will teach you better about life and human nature than waiting tables or flipping burgers for a year or two."

"Agreed."

"My mom's always worked those jobs," she explains. "She just has her high school diploma and had to take whatever would be flexible enough to raise me. And then I'd get sick and she'd have to take time off and sometimes get fired for it. Then she'd start the whole thing over again, finding another job."

"She was a single mom?"

"Yeah. My parents divorced when I was a baby and he never took part in anything. I don't think he ever sent us a dime, and it's not like my mom could afford a lawyer to force him to pay."

I frown. "Damn system's broken."

She shrugs. "So anyway, that's why I was so focused on school. I got good grades and scholarships all the way through till I got my masters."

"Was it an MBA?"

She shakes her head. "Political Science. I was pretty settled in DC and figured there was bound to be a place where I could use that there. But I never really thought about finding a career that I loved so much. All I wanted was to just find something stable where I wouldn't always be wondering how I'd pay for the groceries that week."

"And you found it," I observe.

There's a long pause before she answers, "Yeah."

I glance over again at her tone. "You hesitated when you answered."

She rolls her eyes. "Do you notice everything?"

"I'm trained to. I'm a doctor. So, why the hesitation?"

"I, uh—" Her words falter for a moment, and then she shrugs. "I guess nothing's ever as perfect as it seems, right? I love being a lobbyist, but working for a big firm means that I have to push things that sometimes I don't really believe in. You know? If the National Organization of Unicorn Hunters was a client for the firm, then there I'd be, standing up before Congress convincing them that we need to hunt down unicorns. It's kind of mercenary sometimes."

"Fortunately, I doubt they'll be your next client."

"Yeah, unicorn hunting is *so last year*," she says with a laugh. "But if I worked for an organization directly—one that I believe in—then I could have laser sharp focus on it." She turns to me suddenly, seeming a little uncomfortable somehow. "How about you? Did you always want to be a doctor?"

I chuckle. "I'm not even sure. It was my dad who sort of shoved me down that path."

"Really?" She gives me a long once-over. "I'm having a hard time imagining someone could ever *shove* you anywhere."

Taking it as a compliment, I grin. "I was his first born and he really thought that it was my job to sort of... I don't know... be the family success or something. And he thought having a son who was a doctor would somehow make up for the fact that he wasn't the billionaire that his brother was."

She looks at me quizzically until recollection shines in her eyes. "Oh, yeah. Your uncle, the billionaire. Yeah, I imagine that could kind of mess up the family dynamic."

"You have no idea. After Grandpa died and his company went to his kids, Dad and my aunt sold their shares to my uncle. If Dad had kept his piece of the company... well, my high school years would have looked a hell of a lot different." She's easy to talk to, I realize, and imagine that must help her in her career, getting politicians to warm up to her side of the argument.

"Looking back," I find myself continuing, "I think he was depressed for a while over it, back when my uncle really started to reap the profits while we were still trying to make the mortgage in our middle class life. But I was young and didn't see the signs."

For an awkward beat, she's silent before she says, "Some people are really good at hiding those kinds of things."

Something vacant in her tone has me glancing over at her. Her eyes are fixed on some distant point ahead of us and just for a moment, I feel like I'm seeing a side of her she doesn't want to share. "I wish he had told me," I say quietly, and can't help adding, "I'm a good listener."

I put my focus back on the road, hoping she really heard my words. Here in Hawai'i, we have respect for the things that are lying beneath the surface, whether it's marine wildlife below the waves or a lava flow that is poised to erupt. And I can't help feeling like there's something that's hurting her inside.

And since Carl isn't around, I'd like her to know I'm here for her—in a strictly platonic way, of course.

Of course.

"So you gave in and went to medical school," she concludes, her tone suddenly bright again.

"Thanks to the Army, yeah. I majored in pre-med. And once you start down that path, it's a foregone conclusion that you'll end up in either a white lab coat or a strait jacket," I joke. A thought occurs to me as I flick on my turn signal. In all the time I dated Hailey, I'm not even sure if I ever told her about how my father pushed me down the road to medical school. I guess in our relationship there was more *doing* than talking. It's kind of hard to have a heart-to-heart when you're a hundred feet underwater in SCUBA gear or five hundred feet above the water parasailing. "Sometimes I wonder what I would have been if I had a little more of a backbone when I was growing up."

Her eyes widen. "Uh, I've seen those photos of you in uniform. All those medals on your chest tell me you've got one hell of a backbone already."

I laugh. "The Army changes us all."

The smile she sends me is so soothing, so much more serene than when she first stepped off the plane.

Island life looks good on her, I decide. But there's this other side of her that I find just as attractive—that drive and ambition she has that seems to ignite something in me every time I see her.

Her eyes narrow thoughtfully. "It's my theory that, as a parent, you're obligated to mess up your kids in some way. Because otherwise, your kids won't have someone to blame for everything that went wrong with their lives."

"Good theory."

We pull into a tight parking space near the boat dock and unload the beach bags.

Glancing at the shrubs near the car, she furrows her brow. "Huh. Those flowers look like they've been split in half," she notices.

I stop a moment and look down. I love the way she notices things about the island that I take for granted after living here a while. "Oh, yeah. That's the naupaka kahakai."

Her brow rises. "You never cease to amaze me. So you're a lava expert *and* a horticulturist?"

I laugh. "Hardly. Everyone knows that flower here. There's a legend about it."

"Okay, so now you've intrigued me. I hope you're going to share."

I nearly cringe. I hate butchering a legend with my poor storytelling skills. "I'll try. But I might get parts wrong."

She tilts her head. "Do you really think a girl from DC will notice?"

Hoisting a beach bag on each of my shoulders, I sigh. "Okay. There are lots of different versions of this. But the way it was told to me is that there was this man. Young guy. And *Pele*—you know, the goddess—she found him attractive. But he was already in love with someone else."

She frowns. "I can already tell there's no happy ending."

"Right. So, she's angry about it, and she chases him up into the mountains. *Pele*'s sisters see this and they know she'll kill him. So to save him, they turn him into the mountain naupaka, which looks pretty similar to this. With a half flower, you know."

"I can already guess—then *Pele* goes after the girl he loved, right?"

"Exactly. She chases her down to the sea. And *Pele*'s sisters save her by turning her into this." I give a nod toward the flowers along the pathway as we walk.

Her face elongates. "Couldn't *Pele* have just killed the flowers, then?"

I chuckle because I had the same thought when I heard the story. "You're not much of a romantic."

"I've never had a reason to be," she says a little woefully. Stopping for a moment, she bends slightly, taking a closer look before resuming our walk. "And if you bring the two flowers together? Does *Pele* get angry?"

My smile fades thoughtfully, admiring her logic because her brain seems to work the same way mine does. "You know, that would make sense, wouldn't it? But actually, I was told that the lovers would be reunited."

She grins, almost whimsically—and the expression is something that I just can't picture on her face in the middle of the pressure cooker that DC is. "I like that thought better," she decides.

Me, too. I want to say it, but I don't, for some reason thinking the notion is a little too sentimental for a guy like me.

They have so many legends on this island, I'd thought I had become immune to them.

Yet telling her the story somehow tugs something in my heart, because when I'm with her, I can almost relate to the idea that there's a half of each of us that is missing, just like with the flower. And it's up to us to find our other half in someone else.

Samantha makes me remember a side of myself that I've missed living out here in paradise—the ambition, the commitment to my career that used to define me before I left the military. And when I'm with her, I feel just a little more complete.

And that's the wrong feeling to have with this woman.

CHAPTER 8

~ SAMANTHA ~

"Need some help on your back?"

I stiffen at Dodger's words as I contort my torso, struggling to smear the thick reef-safe sunscreen provided by the boat's crew.

Did he really just ask that with the deep, imposing timbre of his sexy as hell voice? Or am I in some fantasy, bouncing around on a boat bathed by sunlight with the profile of Hawai'i in the distance?

I glance over my shoulder at him.

I *hate* that I *do* need help with my back. Because I know that when I nod my answer... and feel his hands on my skin... I'll be feeling things for this man that I simply shouldn't.

And I'm right.

My skin practically sizzles at his touch and a blush casts itself over my body as my nipples harden. It shouldn't be like this. I knew what the guy looked like when I agreed to stay with him, and I thought I could resist. But the trouble is, the way he talks, the way he listens, the way he inexplicably meshes with me, notches his sexiness factor up to heights I really can't handle.

I pray for a cool breeze—some excuse so that when I turn around to face him, he won't know what his touch is doing to me. He won't know that with one touch, he's aroused me more than Carl did in two years of dating.

But no breeze comes. So when he's done, I quickly order him, "Turn around. I'll do the same for you."

Big mistake.

Colossal mistake.

Because I've never in my life touched muscles as hard and broad as Dodger's. Suppressing a purr, my hands glide over the hills and valleys of his back all the way down to wear the waistband of his swim trunks dares me—*dares* me to dip lower. When I'm just there, I see his back straighten slightly and he turns promptly.

Our eyes meet, and for a moment I can't help thinking that our thoughts are the same—that right now, we both want something that we shouldn't.

I must be imagining it. He's got someone. She's gorgeous and smart. And even more, she's so nice that she not only lets me stay with her boyfriend, she even helped make my trip more memorable yesterday.

I feel ashamed of these hormones that urge me to knock this man onto his back right now and have my way with him, even on a boat we share with about thirty other people.

What the hell is wrong with me?

"Dolphins!" someone cries out, and immediately dozens of pairs of feet scurry to the portside of the huge catamaran. I follow—not because the excitement of seeing a dolphin exceeds the surge I'm feeling deep in my core from being near Dodger. I follow because I need to get away from him.

When I reach the rail, I spot the dolphins—an entire pod following our boat, leaping in the wake we leave behind us.

Elated, I cry out like a little kid each time one soars out of the water and plunges in again. Seeing something like this in person is so different from watching it on YouTube or TV, and my eyes soak in the sight of it.

"I was hoping you'd get to see this," he says, suddenly behind me. Immediately, my breath catches with him so close that I can feel the warmth of his body.

"Does this happen a lot?" I ask, unable to pull my eyes from the dolphins.

"Actually, yeah, it does. The dolphins seem to enjoy jumping in the wake."

"I've always loved dolphins," I admit, feeling as though I'm a different person as I watch them—someone who doesn't even own a cell phone or obsess over my career or ponder the stressors of the life I've carved out for myself.

Right now, I'm free. Free of it all.

"Who *doesn't* love dolphins?" he counters.

"Good point."

"If we get really lucky, we might see them in the bay when we're snorkeling. Just remember not to approach them."

"They're protected. Marine Mammal Protection Act." Glancing over my shoulder, I add in my fake know-it-all tone, "I do learn a few things lobbying in DC, you know."

I take in the sight of him as he laughs, standing there with the breeze tossing his short hair and the sun kissing his tanned skin.

Lucky sun.

Yes, I may have learned a few things in DC. But right now, all my body seems interested in are the things this man could teach me—and not just in the bedroom. I want to know how he became so at ease with himself and his life, how everything he does seems to mirror the serenity of the ocean waves as they caress the shoreline.

Is everyone in Hawai'i like this? I'm almost embarrassed to admit that it took three visits to this island for me to even notice such a thing.

We anchor in Kealakekua Bay within sight of the Captain Cook Monument, its obelisk shape reminding me of the Washington Monument back home, but just in a much smaller size. I would have expected a pang of nostalgia at the thought—some vague urge to return to the stately, historic buildings and energy that I love about DC. Yet right now, after I step to the back of the boat, my thoughts are only of Hawai'i and this man as I slip on the flippers the boat crew had given me.

Sharks or not, I might follow Dodger anywhere.

"It's freezing!" I exclaim as I start to step off the boat, the chilly water feeling frigid against skin that's been heated in the sun.

"Not once you get all the way in. Promise."

Sucking in a breath, I jump off the last step of the boat's swim platform and toward him, letting out a gasp at the cold. "L-l-l-liar!" I stutter.

"Give it a minute. Just pull your mask over your eyes and look under us."

"I'm not putting my face in this! T-t-too cold."

"If you regret it in the slightest after you see what's under there, I will personally pay your rent next month."

I sputter. He looks dead serious as he says it, but I can't imagine he is. Still, that's an offer an unemployed woman can't refuse. "It's all bets and dares with you, isn't it?"

His grin is devilish. "Grew up in a house with two brothers. It was all bets and dares and pranks. I might be putting a bug in your hair before the day is out."

"So mature."

"Stop delaying and put your face in."

Narrowing my eyes on him momentarily, I pull down my mask and stick the snorkel in my mouth the way Dodger showed me earlier. I dip my face under the waterline.

Oh my....

I hear a thrilled squeal, muffled from behind a snorkel and I don't even realize at first that it's me. I'm that enthralled.

Pure, unrelenting beauty reveals itself to me beneath the waves. I'm in awe at the life that exists down here. Yellow and black striped fish with angular shapes, plump pink ones with a hue of blue when the light strikes them. Others are long and skinny with needle-like noses that make them look like the ocean's stunning version of hummingbirds. With every kick of my flippers, I'm propelled further into something so exquisite I'd think I'm in a dream.

I saw *Finding Nemo* when I was a kid like the rest of the world. So I grew up knowing that the ocean was capable of beauty like this. Yet I assumed the animators must have taken some liberty.

Yet nothing I've seen could possibly recreate the vibrant colors and diversity that I'm looking at now. Lured by the sight of the reef and the anemones and sea urchins that are embedded in it, I swim curiously in its direction. A wave starts pushing me more quickly toward it than I can fight, and panic sets in.

A hand grasps mine. It's Dodger—quite apparently a stronger swimmer than me because he pulls me to a safer distance. I try to let go of his hand then; it seems too intimate. But he holds tight, taking me around the reef on a guided tour that I wouldn't trade a month of paychecks for, hands-down.

If I had a paycheck, that is.

On our journey, he points out sea life as we encounter it —even spotting two turtles approaching us. He stops our movement at that, giving them a wide berth as they pass. Some larger fish, one seeming almost translucent and the other as metallic as a sheet of foil, approach us. If I knew all the names of these creatures, I could look up photos online and show people back home what I was lucky enough to see. Yet even if they saw it on my computer, they'd never quite appreciate it the way I can right now.

Here, I feel like I'm part of an entirely different plane of reality—the same as I did when I was lying out under those stars the other night, or standing on hardened lava, fresh land that had just been created by the earth itself.

And I owe it to Dodger. Even with the beauty around me, I can't help glancing at him, the sinewy curves of his muscles somehow accentuated by the way the sun shines through the water. Without him, I'd be sitting in his condo, digging for jobs online and retreating to his bathroom from time to time for a good hard cry while the world continued to turn on its axis.

I'd be missing out on so much.

I'm nearly numb by the time the boat horn blows, calling us back. Numb—not from the cold, but from this dream-like state I'm in.

I'm in love with Hawai'i. And if I don't watch myself, I could easily fall in love with Dodger—this man whose hand is still holding mine as he helps me out of the water.

"So, am I paying your rent?" he asks.

"My what? Oh—I forgot." Of course I had forgotten his joke that he'd pay my rent if I regretted this. "You're definitely off the hook on that. It's gorgeous under there."

After handing me a towel, his muscles tighten as he moves to wipe himself down, making for a hell of a sight.

When he looks up, I feel myself blush as he catches my appreciative stare.

He grins. "You'll forget a lot more after I get you one of the drinks they serve on this boat. They've got a margarita that Hailey said is the best she's ever tasted. And she's a connoisseur."

Hailey. Crap. How easy it is to forget about her. For me, anyway. I'm a bad, bad person.

I'm going straight to hell.

My eyes follow Dodger as he heads to the boat's small bar, enjoying too much the way his swim trunks fall low on his hips.

Yep. Straight to hell. But what a view I've got along the way.

CHAPTER 9

- DODGER -

For someone who's supposed to be the smartest of our trio of brothers, I'm feeling like an idiot.

I'm *still* feeling that way, twelve hours later, after diagnosing a handful of viruses of various sorts, a couple ear infections, five or so rashes from different plants we've got here, and stitching up a pretty major gash on someone who tripped over a pool toy.

I might be a suitable urgent care doc, but I'm still an idiot.

I lift myself into my Jeep and grip my steering wheel, staring out to the dark skies while the quiet consumes me, just long enough to hear the voice in my head reminding me that I was a fool to take Samantha out on that boat today.

My clinic is on Mauna Lani Drive just off the Queen K Highway, a location that looks desolate when I get off my night shift, and only slightly less so in the daylight. Truth is, the landscape here—vast swaths of undeveloped, hard lava

—can look a little off-putting to some people until they drive off the highway and discover pockets of stunning beauty.

Tonight, the quiet that greets me in the small parking lot only lets my brain fall into the same pattern it's been in since we stepped onto that damn boat.

It drifts to Samantha, lingers for a while on the memory of how it felt to hold her hand as I swam with her, and then does a sharp turn at that point when I remember Carl and his damn phone.

This might be easier if he wasn't such a titwad.

"Idiot." I actually say it out loud this time, not at the thought of Carl, but of me, chastising myself for creating this situation in the first place.

Taking her snorkeling meant that I got to rub lotion on her back under the pretense of skin protection. Taking her snorkeling meant that I got to hold her hand to keep her a safe distance from the coral. Taking her snorkeling meant that I got to give her a margarita and see how gorgeous she looks when her eyelids fall to half-mast at the feel of tequila in her veins.

How is it that when I'm with Samantha, I feel more chemistry after a few days together than I did with Hailey after nearly a year of trying?

My brothers, now that they're happily married, can utter words like destiny and kismet without even cracking a smile. I blame their wives because they were never like this before marital bliss.

Me? The doctor, the *scientist* in me likes the quantifiable—experiments that a person can replicate. I prefer logic over things like destiny.

And logic reminds me that Samantha has a boyfriend waiting for her back home, not to mention a job she clearly adores.

Why can't I ever feel this level of attraction for someone who wants to stick around?

Thank God she doesn't cook. That would do me in.

Snapped out of my reverie when two of my nurse practitioners wave as they head to their cars, I pull out my phone to check for texts from Cam about Baby K and Annie. But no news is good news in that pocket of this island, so I back out of my space and head home.

The lights are on when I pull in, and I can't deny that there's a part of me that enjoys the sight of it. Still outside, I kick off my shoes, open the door and...

Holy crap.

"What's that smell?" I immediately blurt. Not *"Hello."* Not *"How was your evening?"*

Just *"What is that smell that is unlocking images of my childhood that I thought I'd forgotten?"*

"Oh, hi!" Barefoot, she's standing in shorts and a t-shirt stirring something with a wooden spoon and looking like the most desirable woman on the planet to me.

It's gotta be the smell.

No. It's more than that.

"I couldn't sleep again," she says, grinning. "So I thought I'd whip something up for you."

"That *something* is the stuff of fantasies. I thought you said you couldn't cook." My mouth waters as I come up behind her and stare into the pot.

"Oh, I can't. But this is the one thing my mom made me learn how to make before I left for college. She swears a good homemade chicken soup can cure anything."

"There are actual studies about that," I can't help pointing out. I lean over the pot—a pot, I might add, that hasn't been used in years—and inhale every memory of cold Ohio winters when my mom would make hot soup and top it with homemade dumplings. "I love your mother," I add.

She grins. "That makes two of us."

"You didn't have to do this. You should be in bed." And just like that, the word *bed* seems to edge out those innocent childhood memories I was enjoying.

Filthy mind.

"Still have jetlag?" I ask.

"I don't think so. I just had such an adrenaline rush from the snorkeling. After you left for work, I drove around a bit, discovered Foodland, and stocked up on what I needed. I wasn't even sure if you'd be hungry when you got home, but this stores really well. I actually keep some in my freezer all the time, just in case I get sick and don't have the energy to make it. Here," she says, ladling some into a bowl for me.

"If it tastes half as amazing as it smells, I'm yours forever." There's humor in my tone, but still, I regret letting it slip.

"That would be awkward," she rebuts, most certainly thinking of how she'd explain that to Carl.

Oh, don't worry. I could find innumerable ways to make that guy disappear. Just give me the chance.

After giving it a quick stir, she puts the lid back on the pot. "I probably made too much. You can live off it for a week." She lets out an awkward laugh. "Does Hailey like chicken soup?"

My brow furrows at the odd question. I know Hailey and I parted ways amicably, but it's not like I enjoy her name being brought up every time I start feeling something I shouldn't for Samantha.

"She's vegetarian," I answer.

"Oh." She looks strangely disappointed in my answer. "Well, how about you sit down? You must be tired." She tosses her chin in the direction of the counter.

"It's nice out. Let's eat on the lanai," I suggest, and when she agrees, I pour her a glass of wine and juggle it, along with my bowl and a bottle of beer.

The fresh, brisk air is welcome to me, cooling me down. Standing in the hot kitchen with Samantha, I was too close to the stairs. And the stairs lead to my room. And there's a bed in my room.

A big one, built for two.

Get a handle on yourself, Dodger.

As she steps outside, I turn to see her backlit by the glow from my living room lights. I start to think this was my *second* bad idea of the day.

Damn, she's beautiful. Dark tresses caress her shoulders, with gentle wisps framing her delicate face. I'd pay good money for the right to just tuck those loose tendrils behind her ears—any excuse to touch her again and see if I feel that same spark I always do.

Only because experiments need replicating, of course.

"It's always nice out here," she barely whispers it, as if she doesn't want to break the stillness of the night.

"Just about."

"Do you ever tire of it?"

"No. But sometimes I wonder if I appreciate it as much as I should." I take a spoonful into my mouth. "Oh my God, this is so good."

"I'm glad you like it. You were saying about the weather..." She prods me to continue almost as though she's uncomfortable receiving praise about her cooking skills.

"The weather, yeah." I can't resist taking another spoonful before I continue. "Um, the good thing about having *bad* weather from time to time is that you really notice the better weather more when it comes. Here, I kind of miss opening up my window in the morning and feeling that element of surprise because, well, it's almost always like this."

"I never thought about that. I guess you need some bad things in life to make you appreciate the good."

There's a glimmer of sadness in her eyes when she says it,

and it takes me right back to earlier today when we were driving in the car and she had the same look of emptiness.

Again, it makes me wonder what's bad in her life because all I want to do right now is fix it for her. I can't help wondering if Carl would do the same. And somehow, I know instinctively he's too absorbed in his own life to notice shit about what's happening in his girlfriend's life.

I didn't like the guy before. But I'm finding my contempt for him ratchets upward each time I see anything but happiness in Samantha's eyes. Because she deserves better.

Better than him.

"Sometimes you need to slow down in life to realize things like that," I offer cautiously.

Now she graces me again with the smile I love to see from her.

"Dodger, haven't you caught on? I'm not too good at slowing down."

Contemplating, I lean back as I take another spoonful. "I was like that back when I lived in DC. It's the culture there."

"Yeah. I used to feel naked without my cell phone."

Naked. Did she really have to say that? "I can't help noticing you said *used to*." I grind out the reply trying to purge the image of her naked from my brain.

"I guess Hawai'i is having some effect on me. Back home, I can't imagine introducing myself without handing out my business card. Here? Not so much."

"Yeah, you'd get a few odd looks if you did. And a little piece of paper can't really define a person." I devour another bite, suppressing the urge to propose marriage, because this soup is just that delicious. "That was one of the first things I noticed here," I say instead. "In DC, people think you're a success by how much you work. Here, it's by how much you get to play."

"That's the way it should be, though, shouldn't it?" she offers thoughtfully.

I shrug. "Honestly, I kind of miss the days when I took my career more seriously."

"You're a doctor. That sounds pretty serious to me."

"I fix up tourists. A few stitches here and there. A lot of colds and sunburns. Half of them just see me because they got sick on their vacation and want a note they can send to their travel insurance company so they can get their money back for needing to extend their trip."

"Really?"

"Yep. I get about three of those every day. Makes me feel like a teacher handing out hall passes." I frown. "It's not the same way I felt when I was an Army doc, believe me."

"That must have been a lot more intense."

"Exactly. Opposite of here. I miss it sometimes."

"Were you always stationed in the DC area?"

"No. Most of the time I was in the Middle East. I'd volunteer for those posts so that some other doctor who's got a wife and kids stateside could stay with them. I'm a single guy, right? Doesn't really matter that I miss a few Christmases. Though don't tell my mom I said that."

She laughs. "I won't."

"Besides, my brothers were generally out that way. And even though we'd rarely get a chance to meet up, I liked being close by. You know, just in case. Fen was always doing medevac, and Cam was with the Rangers. I bounced around a lot."

"Join the Army. See the world. Isn't that what they say?"

"See the world with body armor and a sidearm sometimes," I chuckle. "My last post was at Walter Reed. I was a pain management specialist there. I liked that job the most."

"Why's that?"

"For a job that was stateside, it was the most challenging. I felt like I made a difference. A lasting one."

"What does a pain management specialist do exactly?"

"The military—it's invented a million ways to break the human body. Patients came to me when nothing else was working for their pain. And it's a long-term relationship we're in because, especially these days, with addiction to pain meds such a problem, people need monitoring. They need someone who takes the time to learn their background, to find out what's happening in their homes and at their jobs because all of that has an impact. You have to get to know someone well before you figure out what might work best with their lifestyle."

She scoffs quietly. "I'm trying to remember the last time a doctor took the time to get to know me."

"That's just it. They often don't," I tell her. "But they should, and they really have to when it comes pain. One thing works for you, but another thing works for someone else, even if your symptoms seem identical. And there's a lot of trial-and-error involved." I can't help noticing how much I'm enjoying this—talking about my past line of work.

"It's like a mystery you need to solve."

I nod, surprised she gets it. "Exactly. I'd develop an instinct about my patients after a while. I'd know a medication or a therapy would have a chance before even trying it."

"That sounds like a good talent to have when you're a doctor."

"That's just it, though. It's not a talent. It just happens when you take the time to get to know your patients." My lips tighten into a thin line for a moment. "Then they made me move."

Her brow creases. "Is that why you got out of the Army?"

"Yep. It really pissed me off. The Army is like a big machine. You can talk to commanders—they might get it.

But when the Army says it's time to move, they'll make you go, even if it's not what's best for your patients. They don't care that the things I know in my gut about my patients aren't things that I can just jot down on a chart and hand over to the next doc."

"That must have been hard. Finally, being in a job you loved and then being forced to leave." She says it as though she's had some personal experience in that department.

"Yeah. It was." Again, it strikes me how easy it is to just *talk* with Samantha. Opening up to a woman like this doesn't come easily to me. I theorize it comes from being raised in a house that was overflowing with testosterone.

It makes me want to cancel the date I've got lined up tomorrow night just so I can spend the time with Samantha instead, even if she *is* taken by someone else.

I feel myself sink deeper into my seat, finally completely unwinding. I enjoy being with her like this, just sitting here with no expectations other than the enjoyment of each other's company. "Looking back, I don't know if I even did the right thing, leaving the Army like that. But it was just after Cam and Fen got out, and it seemed like the thing to do. And when I saw there weren't many docs in this area, I got together with a couple other M.D.s and opened the doc-in-a-box."

"Doc-in-a-box." She grins, taking another sip of her wine. "I've never heard that one before."

"It pretty much sums it up. It's good work, don't get me wrong. And I like that being here means that the ERs are a little less clogged up by tourists who don't have big emergencies. That makes it a little easier for locals to get care. Just this year, a few docs on Maui took up our brand and opened our first franchise over there, and I was just contacted by someone last week about doing the same thing on Kaua'i."

"Wow. Congratulations."

"Thanks. So I guess I can eye an early retirement." I should be excited at the prospect. But then I look again at her, remembering that light in her eyes when she talks about her work, that passion that she seems to have which was lost to me at some point these past years.

I realize that I want that for myself.

No, more than that. I want *her* for myself.

To hell with Carl.

CHAPTER 10

~ SAMANTHA ~

I'm normal. That's what I need to remind myself right now.

It's perfectly normal to find a man like Dodger attractive.

It's perfectly normal—even though he has a girlfriend—to notice the subtle curve of his lips and wonder what it might feel like to have them touch me. It's normal to notice in the low light the sharp angles of his face or the way his muscular form looks almost menacing as he stands up to take our bowls into the kitchen. Menacing, until he smiles in that way that makes my breath catch.

I'm a woman the same as any other. I know my reaction to him is normal.

What's *not* normal is my desire to act on what I'm feeling. I think of Hailey—of how she doesn't seem to mind that I'm here in Dodger's house, enjoying his hospitality, his company, his... *everything* since I got here a few days ago. If I was Hailey, I don't know if I'd be that trusting, that generous.

But I'm not Hailey.

"You're going to bed?" I ask as he turns toward the sliding glass door. Why is it that the question seems lacking innocence when my core feels so warm?

He shakes his head. "No. I'll just load the dishwasher and come back out. It takes me a while to wind down from work sometimes."

I'd swear his gaze lingers on me a beat longer than it should. But he's tired. That's all it is.

"Let me get those." I eye the bowls as I start to stand.

"No, I've got them." He heads inside.

I should follow him and insist. I made the mess. I need to clean it up. Yet the idea of standing in that kitchen with him is not a good one. It's a good sized kitchen for a condo, but it would be too easy to succumb to temptation—too easy to lightly brush my body against his as I reach for the sink or accidentally lean against him when I open the dishwasher.

No, I'll just stay right here where the night breeze blowing off the ocean can cool me down. Where the distance between us should provide some measure of relief.

Maybe this was a mistake, greeting him with a meal this late at night after a day that will easily be remembered as one of the best in my life. Because it's not chicken soup I want to offer him to repay him for his hospitality.

No, it's definitely not.

Relax, dammit. I press my eyelids shut, breathing in with the sound of every wave that rolls in, and out again as I hear it recede. In. Out. In. Out. In...

"Pretty moon."

... and just like that, my body tenses up again as he comes up behind me.

"Yeah." I somehow manage a strangled reply as he sits again. There's dead silence between us as we stare out, and it feels too comfortable. Too romantic. As though the best way to fill that silence right now would be to lean over and offer my lips to him. My lips… as just a beginning.

"Do you miss the change of seasons?" I crank out instead. Hey, it's not much, but it's all I've got.

It's dark and the moon is barely a sliver in the sky tonight, so all I can see are the whitecaps as they roll in and then vanish when they hit the shore. Just the whitecaps—and him in my peripheral view, lifting his chin slightly and turning toward me. But I don't dare meet his eyes.

"Who says we don't have a change of seasons here?" he asks lightly.

"I do. You can't tell me all these palm trees turn orange and drop their leaves in the fall," I joke.

"Our seasons are just different." His gaze on me makes me sizzle inside, even when I'm not looking at him. This man is nothing short of dangerous.

"We know that winter is coming when the whales start to arrive," he says in that logical tone he uses from time to time. "Then in spring, you start missing them and counting the days till they return."

I venture to look at him then. His eyes are contemplative, seeming to follow the outline of my face and for a brief moment, his gaze rests on my lips.

Oh my. Could we be on the same page here?

And doesn't that make this twice as dangerous?

"How about summer? Are there any tells?" I follow-up, curious.

"Sure. You know it's summer because the water is at its calmest. Though it kind of depends on where you are on the island, so you always should be cautious."

I laugh. "I've noticed that everything you say comes with a big disclaimer."

"Yeah. That's the doctor in me. Cam and Annie always say everything out of my mouth is preceded by a big asterisk."

I suck in a breath. "Oh, speaking of Cam and Annie, I heard from them today and they're doing much better. They even invited me over for dinner tomorrow night. So it sounds like I might finally get out of your hair."

"You're not in my hair."

"I am," I insist.

"You're not."

"Dodger, I'm sleeping in your house, eating your food, consuming your time, and you won't even let me pay for anything."

"You made me soup. No one I know makes chicken soup on this island. We're even." He glances over his shoulder toward the kitchen. "No, considering how good that was, the scales are actually tipped in your favor."

There's an odd pause between us, so I reach for my wine just to occupy my hands with something. Because it's him I want to reach for.

Finishing off the last of my drink, I give myself a shake. "Cam says he's making loco moco tomorrow night. I have no idea what that is."

"You'll love it."

"You should join us," I suggest.

He looks like he's about to say yes, until his face sags slightly. "No. I've got plans tomorrow night."

Of course. Hailey. "Bring her along," I suggest. Even though I know that seeing them together is the last thing I want, it might be just what I need to throw some water on this fire burning in me.

"No. You guys have fun. And if you change your mind and want to stay here rather than there, my door's always open."

Not the right thing to say to a woman who would love to slip into your bed tonight, buddy. I pull my eyes from his and stand to head inside. But I can't resist glancing over my shoulder. Not at him again—I'd swear it. Just at the moon.

"I always forget what they call that kind of moon. You know, when it's just a sliver like that," I say. I don't know why I said it, because I've never really given the matter any thought until now. But there's this part of me that fights the idea of going inside, as though I want to feel this—this closeness with him—even if it is just an illusion.

"Waxing crescent," he answers, his gaze on it joining mine. "If the crescent was facing the other way, it would be a waning crescent."

I look at him as he stands, and am reminded again why I shouldn't. God, he looks so tempting on a night like this. "Is that something else you learned about since moving here? Kind of like tsunami zones and types of lava?"

He looks uncertain. "Not really sure where I picked that up."

"Well, it's pretty," I say just as a cool breeze tosses my hair in a million different directions. Damn trade winds, I think, somehow not wanting to spend my last moments with him tonight looking disheveled.

He traces a finger along my face, exposing my eyes from the wisps of hair and tucks a lock behind my ear. "Very pretty," he murmurs.

Oh.

Oh no.

I don't know which one of us started to close the space between us to barely an inch. Probably me. Possibly him. I only know that at this proximity, the pull between us is magnetic, impossible to fight. And it's me—it's definitely me who stands up on my tiptoes needing to be even closer until I feel my lips suddenly against his.

My sharp intake of breath seems to echo his own, both of us stunned that we now find ourselves melded together, yet unwilling to pull back. Not yet, because all reason has escaped me. Instead, I savor the feel of him, angling my face as he threads his fingers into my hair, easing me further upward with one hand. His heat through the cotton of his shirt seems to scorch me, and when my lips yield to him, he slips his tongue into me.

I nearly come undone.

Instinct takes over, desperate, pressing myself against him. My core aches, wanting him so badly, wanting to feel him inside me as though I've been missing a piece of myself until just now—just now when I've finally found what I need to fill the void.

Literally.

My muscles tighten, nails digging into his back as I urge him closer to me, even though there's already not a breath of space between us. With his chest pressed against me, I can feel his heartbeat—its rapid-fire cadence reflecting mine. I want this, this kiss, this strong hold he has me in, this feel of his arms enveloping me. But I want more.

Breathing in his musky scent, I splay my hands across his back, savoring the feel of his muscles underneath my fingertips. He nearly growls in response, with one of his hands now at the nape of my neck and the other at my hip, holding me as though he'll never let go.

Until he does.

Spine suddenly straightening, his lips leave mine and I nearly cry out from the absence of them.

"Holy shit."

I think he said it. I'm not sure because my brain is as weak as my legs which are about to give out from beneath me.

But the words are the slap of reality I need. "Oh, crap, Dodger. I'm so sorry."

"No—no, that one was on me, really."

"It wasn't." I picture Hailey, somewhere on this island,

snuggled into her bed, thinking her boyfriend is safe with the likes of me. I've broken the Girl Code.

Stick a scarlet letter on my chest and send me on the first plane home.

He shakes his head. "I'm a foot taller than you. You couldn't reach up to my lips unless you sprouted wings. That was my doing. Dammit, Samantha, I'm sorry."

But it *wasn't* him. I know it. It was me.

"No, Dodger. Believe me when I say it was me. And just— the moon. The wine. And I was tired."

"Yeah. Yeah. Me, too. But my behavior was uncalled for."

"Well, right back atcha," I mutter, so angry with myself for my lack of control. "Look, I'll definitely be out of here tomorrow, okay? If Annie can't take me, I'll get a hotel. This is just not right."

"Don't rush out because of this."

"I should, anyway. You've been way too generous. With your time. Your condo." With your lips, I feel the urge to add. Such generous lips.

He looks deflated. "I understand."

"We—we better get to bed. Separately," I add, then cringe, feeling like a fool for stating the obvious. What is it about this man that makes my brain short circuit?

"Yeah. Again, I'm sorry."

"It was my fault. Can we just…forget this happened? I don't want to mention it to Annie." I don't bother asking him to hold it back from Hailey. Dodger doesn't strike me as the type to keep secrets from his girlfriend. Damn him for being so perfect.

"Of course. Whatever you want. I—uh—"

"Good night," I cut him off, backing away quickly and then, walking right into the sliding glass door.

"Oh, shit." He grabs me as I stumble backwards straight into his arms.

And oh… it feels so good.

"Are you okay?"

My head throbs. "I'm fine."

"No. You hit your head. Let me look at that." He cups my face in one hand and strokes his fingers along where my skull smacked against the glass.

I tug myself away. Clearly I don't have a concussion or my body wouldn't be responding to his touch like this. Or at least I don't *think* it would. "Really. F-fine. I'm fine." I stumble over my words the same way I just stumbled into his arms. "Although I clearly shouldn't drink under the moonlight when I'm still jetlagged."

That's it. Blame jetlag. *Liar.*

"I'll just head inside now." Stupidly, I reach out through the doorway this time to make sure I'm not headed for the glass again.

"Samantha, again, I'm really—"

"Sorry—I know. Me, too."

And yet, I realize as I dart away from him and retreat behind my closed bedroom door, I'm *not* sorry.

Because at thirty years old, I've never experienced something like that in my life. That feeling like destiny might be more than something people talk about in Hallmark movies that I'd never admit to watching. It feels exquisite and unique and life-changing—to even know that I'm capable of this feeling… to even know that such a thing exists. So how could I be sorry?

Until I remember Hailey.

CHAPTER 11

- DODGER -

"So how long have you been a poet?"

Ah, the things I thought I'd never have to ask a woman.

Never say never.

After a busy day at the clinic, I should appreciate this evening, drinking a bourbon while watching the sun set over A-Bay with a remarkably stunning woman. And while I never thought I'd go on a date with a poet, I consider myself just enough of a Renaissance man that I should find the idea intriguing.

Yet after last night with Samantha, *she's* the only thing I find intriguing.

"Since I was eight years old," my date, Katriana, answers. She asked me out for a drink after a brief conversation at Foodland about a week ago. And while I didn't expect to have much in common with her, the woman did know how to pick out a perfectly ripe star fruit.

That has to count for something.

"Eight years old," I repeat back to her, trying desperately to sound impressed by that. "Wow. That's a long time." Silently, I berate myself for not canceling this date. Even if she *was* the perfect woman for me, I doubt I'd notice it right now. But canceling last-minute isn't my style, unless there's an emergency. By necessity, I jerked around enough women doing that while I was an Army doc and my schedule would change on a dime. I'm not about to revert to my old ways when I have no excuse except the desire to spend my evening with a woman who already has a boyfriend.

Even if he is lacking any redeeming qualities by my measure.

"It is a long time." Her eyes flash with pride, God bless her. "I just published my sixteenth volume of poetry last summer and am working on my next one now. That's why I moved here. It's so inspiring. Do you like poetry?"

I chuckle. "I have two brothers. The only poetry I heard growing up started with 'There once was a girl from Nantucket.'"

The light in her eyes dims. She's clearly not impressed. And considering I should probably try a little harder, I toss in, "Though I have read some William Butler Yeats."

"You like Yeats?" Her lashes flutter.

"A bit, yeah, I do. Though if my Irish ancestors are listening, I'll tell you I read him every day."

Her gaze on me shifts to approving again. "It's so pretty here at night."

"It is," I agree, my mind immediately drifting to the beauty of last night, with barely a sliver of the moon and Samantha in my arms. Which is exactly where my mind shouldn't be right now. "How long have you been on-island?" I force myself to ask.

"Three months. I'm planning on sticking around, though."

Considering my track record with women leaving, that should sound promising to me. "Sure you won't get island fever and leave?"

"Island fever?"

"Yeah. It's what we call it when people start getting tired of being so far away from anything else."

She shakes her head adamantly. "No. I'm used to island life. I lived on Manhattan for three years."

"Manhattan," I repeat, pausing for a beat. "You mean New York City?" I somehow need to specify.

"Yes. It's an island."

I feel my mouth gape slightly. "Well, yeah. But it's kind of different, wouldn't you say?" I feel the necessity to point out.

"Not really. Everything's so expensive there. Just like here. And when you want off, it's a real pain."

"It's a short subway ride off Manhattan," I offer, having made many trips out that way.

"I don't take the subway. I just can't relate to the people who use it, you know?"

My eyes widen, trying to wrap my head around whatever convoluted suggestion she's trying to make here. I've always been a big fan of mass transit myself.

"And bridge traffic is terrible," she finishes with an ample sigh that lifts her breasts at least three inches, almost as though she's showing them off.

"But it's easier than a long, expensive plane flight," I rebut, imagining—perhaps wrongly—that a poet's budget must be on the tight side.

She shrugs. "My parents fly Ricky and me out every few months. They miss us."

"Ricky?"

"He's my comfort *companion*." She puts an odd emphasis on the word *companion*.

"Oh. Like, a dog?" I venture to ask.

"Yes. But I'd prefer you didn't call him that," she replies, her eyes now clouded with reprimand.

Check, please.

The instant she sets down her empty glass, my eyes glance around searching for the waitress and sending her the universal hand signal for "*Get me the hell out of here*."

I pull out my credit card and hand it to the waitress without even taking the time to look at the bill. Katriana seems appreciative of the way I snatched it up without question. It might not have been the most promising date I've had, but my rules remain the same.

Unless a woman prefers otherwise, I default to paying.

Some might call it old-fashioned, but it's nothing of the sort. There are three reasons I always pay for dates:

Cramps. Childbirth. Menopause.

Let's face it. Women bear the brunt of keeping our species from going the way of the dinosaur. So if picking up the bill lightens their load even in the slightest, you can be damn sure I won't hesitate to do it.

After I walk her back to her car, I immediately pull my phone out of my pocket to call my brother. I know Samantha moved her things over to their place at some point while I was at work today. And I don't care to admit how empty the house felt when I came home tonight and she wasn't in it.

"Hey, how was the date?" Cam asks immediately.

I'm sure he's asking out of morbid curiosity. "Exactly as you suspect."

"You should have canceled and had dinner with us. Sam loved my loco moco and she even tried Spam musabi."

I smile at the image of it. I'm discovering that I'd smile at *any* image if it included Samantha—which is too strong of a reaction to a woman who has a boyfriend. It really is best she's out of my condo. "Is she all settled in, then?"

"No. I haven't even brought in her bags yet. She and

Annie are out back now with Baby K. I'm still trying to get the house back in order a bit—it looks like a bomb went off in here," he says as though it's Baby K's cold that's to blame, when in fact, it generally looks that way at their house.

"I really wouldn't have minded if she had stayed at my place for longer." Even if *she* would have minded, I can't help thinking. Damn, I really screwed things up between us.

"No, you already came through for us. Keeping Sam busy. Coming out here to check on us. Finding us that new pediatrician, too."

"I'm still just making up for that time I hung you from the doorknob by a wedgie."

"After this, all is forgiven. Hey, why don't you come join us? Have a beer on the lanai."

I ache to say yes. But I imagine I'm the last person Samantha wants to see. All I'll probably remind her of is a kiss that she shouldn't have shared with a man other than her boyfriend.

"Nah. Think I'll just hang at home."

"Suit yourself. So tell me about your date."

"Why? Missing single life?" I ask wryly.

"Hell no. I just like the entertainment you provide."

"Glad my life serves some purpose for you, Bro."

"As bad as all the others?" he assumes.

I don't bother answering. I find I don't need to because he follows up with, "What is it with you and all these first dates that lead nowhere since Hailey left, Dodger?"

"I have a feeling you're about to tell me."

"Well, yeah, I think I can. Look, I remember what it's like to be in your shoes."

Oh, God, save me from this conversation.

"I'd get out there," he continues with his wise-brother tone, "date anyone who happened to come along because, let's face it, we're on an island and the pickings get slim sometimes. But then I end up finding Annie in a parking lot, and she's the babysitter I need for Stella. Hell, if Lancaster hadn't gotten deployed and sent me Stella to take care of for a while, I wouldn't have my wife and kid right now, and even Fen would still be single. Seriously, destiny is better than any singles bar or dating app. Just let it happen, dude."

Destiny, I scoff after ending the call and driving home in blessed silence.

Destiny might have worked for my brothers, and for my cousins before them. But for me, destiny just sent me a woman who's already taken, let me experience the kind of kiss that brings a man to his knees, and then reminded me that I can't have anything more than that.

If I believed in destiny, I'd want to plant my fist in its face.

CHAPTER 12

~ SAMANTHA ~

I'm stretched out on Annie's chaise lounge on her lanai and have a baby sound asleep against my chest. Our infinite universe sparkles above me, and a cool breeze whispers through the palm fronds in the distance.

Before last night's kiss, I might have called this heaven. But this is still a close second.

"Want me to take her?" Annie asks.

I hold my finger to my lips.

Annie smiles. "She won't wake up if we talk. I've found she even sleeps better when there are soft voices around. I think she likes to know she's not alone."

My heart warms for some reason, feeling a kinship with the little tyke. I don't like feeling alone either. Which might be why I put up with Carl for so long.

"She will never be alone, Annie," I murmur. "Too many people love her."

"Well, she sure loves being held by you."

Regretfully, I sigh. "I wish I could come out here more often, Annie. I've been a rotten friend and an even worse godmother."

"What are you talking about? This is your third trip to see me."

"Yeah, but those trips were so rushed." My voice is laced with regret. It had felt too good hugging Annie when I arrived today. Too good, feeling like I have a true friend again, one who doesn't judge me by my lack of a job title or how many useless photos I have of me shaking hands with famous politicians. I've missed her.

"Sam, there are 4,500 miles between us. And you've got such a demanding job."

I sigh. This entire day with Annie, it's been so easy to avoid the topic of work, which is ironic because back home it's all I ever talked about.

Yet here, more important things tend to monopolize the conversation—like tropical fish or lava or starlight or sunrises. Or even more critical, where a person can get freshly made passion fruit juice served in a hollowed out pineapple because it tastes so much better than anything I could ever buy back home.

I should have known I wouldn't be able to avoid the topic of work forever.

"I, uh, *had* a demanding job," I say quietly.

"What? What do you mean, *had*?"

"They lost a couple clients last month. Four of us got laid off."

Annie's face falls. "Oh, no. I'm so sorry."

Gently, with a baby still in my grasp, I shrug.

"Why didn't you tell me, Sam?"

I can't even meet her eyes. "Oh, you know me. I don't like

dumping on people. And you've had so much on your mind with the baby."

"Which means *I've* been the rotten friend. I should have picked up on the fact that there was something wrong."

"No, no. You're not a mind reader. Honestly, I thought I'd get another job quickly and then I'd have *good* news to tell you. And well, you know how it is in DC."

Stoically, she nods. "People define you by what job title you've got."

"Yeah. So I just didn't like to talk about it. Somehow, saying it out loud made it more real to me. And that was the last thing I wanted."

Angling her chin downward, she gazes at me. "I imagine you didn't tell your mom yet either."

"Uh, nooo." I draw out the word as though it's the obvious answer.

She nods and I'm grateful that I don't need to explain to her.

"Has Carl been a support?"

I actually find myself laughing at her question, even with a baby on my chest. Laughing, not crying or even sulking. "Very supportive. So supportive that he dumped me three days after it happened."

Her eyes widen and she takes in a sharp breath. "Son of a b—"

My eyebrows lift. "*Baby,*" I cut her off with the reminder, glancing down at Kaila. "I don't want her first word to be a curse on account of my break up with an a—" Now I catch myself. "—idiot," I finish.

"Wow." She eases back in her chair. "You were with him for so long. I can't even believe he'd do that."

"Well, he was pretty heartbroken." Sarcasm drips from my words.

"Heartbroken?"

"Yeah, there was a big gala that I was going to take him to that Saturday after I got laid off. Lots of potential clients for his law firm. You know him. So anyway, the table at the gala was paid for by Trenton, Leopold, and Wagner, so the poor guy wasn't going to be able to go." I feign a pout.

"How could he bear it?" She matches the scorn in my tone. Then she pauses, eyeing me curiously. "Why do I get the sense that you're not even upset over him leaving you?"

"I think I'm more upset that I wasted so much time on him." My mind drifts to all the tears I've shed these last few weeks, barely able to distinguish which were for Carl and which were for my job.

I rally myself, jutting out my chin proudly. "Besides, let's face it. There was nothing that man was capable of doing for me that I couldn't do myself with far greater efficiency."

She laughs. "You always were practical about love."

Her statement somehow makes me bristle inside.

She's right; I have been too practical in my relationships. And I think I realized it last night, that moment my lips met Dodger's. There's nothing practical about the feelings I have for him. There's nothing practical about daring to feel something for a man whose home is 4,500 miles away from my own. A man who has a girlfriend already. And there's certainly nothing practical in feeling like a kiss can somehow affirm my existence or validate my soul.

Yet despite all that, I want more of it.

So much more.

She tilts her head at my silence, offering the slightest smile that reflects my own. "Maybe you can change that?" she queries lightly.

A couple days ago, I would have met that remark with a quick rebuttal. I would immediately have thought of my mother's infinite counsel on such matters and quoted something like, *"Love is at its best when it's practical."*

Yet somehow, my mother's words just don't fit into this setting, here on an island where anything seems possible.

So instead of speaking, I shift slightly, adjusting the baby's weight in my arms because after an hour of holding her, she feels a lot heavier than what she is.

Annie takes my cue and rises to retrieve little Kaila. As she takes her child back into her arms, she chuckles, "Well, now that I know you're single, I don't know if I should have stuck you at Dodger's place."

I feel myself blush, hoping she can't read my mind right now. "Why do you say that?"

She settles back into her chair. "Poor guy always seems to fall for women like you—women who come to the island and then turn around and leave."

My eyes widen with innocence. Manufactured innocence, to be sure. But it's there just the same. "I wouldn't do that to Hailey," I say quickly. And I'm not lying. Not really. It just depends on what *that* actually is.

Annie cocks her head. "Hailey?"

"Yeah, his girlfriend."

Frowning, she gives her head a slight shake. "Oh, they're not dating anymore."

My chin tucks inward. "Sure they are. She even set us up with a park ranger for when we went to the volcano." I'm surprised that I apparently know more about Dodger's love life than she does. But I guess when you have a baby, keeping track of your brother-in-law falls a little lower on your priority list.

"No, no. Hailey got a transfer with the Park Service. She's working at the Grand Canyon now. They still keep in touch, though. They stayed friends." Her gaze returns to her precious baby as she reflects quietly, "Too bad, really. I actually liked her."

"Wait—what?" I'm immediately digging into my brain for

everything that Dodger said about Hailey, trying to find some indication that it might actually be true. But I come up dry.

"Yeah. She moved just before Fen's wedding. Honestly, looking back, it's almost like they should have just kept things as friends all along. They had all of the same interests, but there just wasn't that…"

"Spark?" I finish for her, immediately thinking of how it felt to touch my lips against his. How it felt to touch him… in any way, actually.

"Yeah," she looks thoughtful. "Yeah. I kind of hope Dodger finds that with someone."

I'm at a momentary loss of words until I barely whisper, "Why didn't you tell me?"

Annie glances at me as though she's already forgotten what we were talking about. "Tell you what?"

"That they broke up!" I blurt, probably too loudly because I watch Kaila stir a little in Annie's arms.

Confused, her brow creases. "Why would I update you on my brother-in-law's dating life?"

She has a point.

I find myself standing, wringing my hands with pent-up sexual frustration. "So hold on a sec. Dodger thinks that I'm dating Carl. And I thought that he was dating Hailey."

She laughs as though the thought just occurred to her, too. "Yeah. Funny!"

Funny? Yeah, it's plenty funny. Funny that I'm still standing here.

Her eyes on me curiously, concern softens her features. "Hey, how about I have Cam bring your luggage in now? You look a little flushed. It takes me a week to get over jet lag. Maybe you should go to bed early."

"No." My response is curt, even though I didn't intend it to be.

"What?"

My mind racing, I stare down at some innocuous speck on the pavers that make up her lanai. "No on the luggage." Then suddenly I look over at her. "And no to going to bed early. At least not—" *Alone*. I nearly actually say it, but cut myself short. "Annie, I know this is going to sound nuts to you, but I have to go."

Her back straightens, worry pinching her eyes. "Home to DC?"

"No. Back to Dodger's." I glance at my watch. "I—I'll explain later. But I promise I'll call you in the morning."

"In the morning? What's going on—oh, *ohhh*..."

Annie's eyes suddenly widen with realization and I almost see a smile.

Almost, because I'm already halfway to her door before I even have time to second-guess myself.

I shouldn't know my way to Dodger's house. I should have needed to punch his address into the GPS on my phone. Yet it's like I'm running on instinct and know exactly how to get there. I could find that man at the end of a maze right now—I'm the mouse and he's the cheese. But it definitely helps that there just aren't too many roads carved into the swaths of hardened lava to get lost here.

It's not until I'm at his door that a thought occurs to me: *He'd said he had plans tonight.*

At the time, I'd assumed it was Hailey. But now that I know the truth, I'm guessing it was a date. A date who might be on the other side of the door right now, getting a hell of a lot luckier than I will if my worries prove to be valid.

But seeing as I've lost my job and my boyfriend, it won't knock me any further down if I lose my dignity tonight.

So I ring the doorbell and am greeted by two heaping eyefuls of man at its best.

He's shirtless with shorts slung low on his hips, just low

enough for me to see that remarkable v of muscles at the base of those glorious abs.

Holy crap. I want to kiss him there.

The sight is even more tantalizing to me now than when we went snorkeling. Amazing how much more tempting a guy is when he's available. And, as my eyes move from side to side looking for his date, I dare to hope that he really *is* available.

Like, *right now*.

"Hi." It's just a word I say. But from my tone, I might as well have said, *"I heard clothing was optional tonight, so thought I'd stop by."*

"Hey." He looks confused. "What are you doing here? Is Baby K okay?"

I'm touched that his first words would show concern for that precious baby. Touched… and aroused as hell from it. Could this guy get any sexier to me?

Then, as he shuts the door behind me, his pecs tense up just enough to give me a show. Yes, he seems to get sexier by the minute.

"She's fine," I reply.

"Did you forget something?"

"No." *Yes. I forgot to have wild, unbridled sex with you.*

"What are you doing here then?"

"Carl dumped me."

His brow creases. "Tonight? Seriously? That bastard."

I reach out to him, daring to touch him on his sculpted forearm almost because he looks like he's about to grab a bag, head to the airport, and go to DC to cold-cock Carl. And while I love the sound of that, it doesn't serve my purpose right now. "No, no. Weeks ago. I—I just didn't get around to telling you."

"You… don't have a boyfriend."

"No." I can't help the slight smile that perks upward on

one side of my mouth. "And I thought you were dating Hailey."

Two distinct lines form on his brow. "No. She left the island over a month ago. I figured you knew that."

I venture to take a step closer, even daring further to move my hand to his chest.

"No," I say, finding myself suddenly breathless. "Annie never told me you two broke it off."

His mouth opens, then snaps shut again as he just stares at me as though he's still letting all this soak in.

"So that means—" I begin again, then cut myself off. "Oh, hell with it," I sigh, figuring sometimes actions speak louder than words.

Feeling reckless, I launch myself at him, propelled by desire that's been building in me for days. Reaching up, I pull his face downward so that I can finally taste him again just like I did last night.

He's decadent to me, like one of those seven-layer cakes in the bakery window you walk by every evening till you finally give in and have to try it for yourself.

His mouth is hot, sizzling against mine as his hands slide down my back. I can feel the muscles in his arms tense up as he pulls me closer, letting me feel the pressure of his erection against me.

Thank God, I can't help thinking. Thank God he wants this, too.

My hands slide against his skin, kneading into his thick, corded muscles and relishing the feel of it. His touch does something to me that defies explanation; my skin seeking out more of this as if it's a life-sustaining sensation.

If he feels this amazing to the touch, I can't even imagine what he'll feel like inside me.

I *have* to find out.

His mouth eases downward to my neck, then to the last

inch of bare skin just above the neckline of my shirt. Giving my t-shirt a little tug, he gathers up a fistful of it in one hand as though he wants the damn thing off me as much as I do.

Breath ragged, his other hand seizes the skin at my waist, pulling me even closer, possessing me.

When he pulls his head away from me for barely an instant, I know he sees panic in my eyes. I don't want him to stop. I don't want him to reconsider. I only want more of this, *right now*, without any thought of whether we'll regret it in the morning. Without any thought of whether this will make our future awkward, the next time I come to this island to see my goddaughter and have to see Dodger again, probably with someone new in his life.

No, I don't want to think about that now.

When he opens his mouth, I somehow worry about what he'll say. *Don't say anything that will make me think right now.*

"Let me make sure I heard all this correctly." His words sound nearly forced. "You're not spoken for."

My heart almost leaps from me, thinking maybe he won't stop this from happening, after all. "Not in the slightest," I confirm.

His eyes flash with desire and I feel nothing but elation from the sight of it.

"You are now," he growls, letting his hands move beneath my shirt, up to the strap of my bra. Then I feel it come undone. And I'm about ready to come undone myself. Our lips find each other again, hot and unyielding with an urgency we seem to share as I stagger backwards a few steps toward his kitchen.

My veins coursing blood that seems to sizzle as it moves through me, I'm in a stupor, pulling him along with me until I'm against the kitchen counter. As I reach down, I feel the throbbing behind the zipper of his shorts. I barely brush him there with my hand and ache with need at the feel of what awaits me.

I'm really doing this. Practical me, throwing myself at a man who can no more fit into my life than this island could. I'm running on instinct alone and it feels heavenly and devilish at the same time.

The idea of that alone has got me in a glorious stupor; I've been waiting too long to thumb my nose at practicality. A fling with a man like this is just what I need to feel desirable again.

Weak suddenly, my knees nearly buckle, and he seems to sense it, lifting me up to sit on his counter. The cool granite on my backside almost makes me shiver in contrast to the heat that's burning inside of me. His tongue slides along my teeth and I savor the taste of him, so clean and masculine with the tiniest hint of Scotch.

"Get this thing off me, Dodger," I say, breath coming in sharp pants as he lifts my shirt from me and then tosses my bra on the floor. What follows is sheer ecstasy—soft lips on my hard nipples and rough hands massaging me in a way that makes me tell him, "I'm way too vertical right now."

His slight laugh vibrates against my breast as he toys with my nipple.

"Upstairs?" he mumbles, barely moving his mouth.

"Too far," I say. Don't make me say more than that. Because all my energy seems to be needed to just savor right now, just savor without passing out cold from the sensations that are consuming me.

I gasp when he lifts me off the counter without missing a beat, his lips still caressing my neck. I feel him move us toward the couch—he's carrying me, I know, but I'd swear I'm floating, until I feel the leather at my back.

I like leather, I decide just then.

I like the way it feels against my skin when I'm so hot like this. I like the way it smells when the aroma combines with a man stretched out over me, pressing his rigidity just where I need it the most.

Heat pools at my center and my pelvis arches instinctively, needing more of the pressure. Needing it so badly I could weep.

I tug at his shorts, demanding him to be completely free of them, and am grateful when he starts to unclasp the button on mine as well.

On top of me, he dominates me, his kisses tracing a path downward to where I need him the most, taking an extra moment to dip his tongue into my navel as he frees me of the last of my clothing. His mouth is ferocious and sweet at the same time, even though I know it's nonsensical to think it. As he moves along my body, his thumbs swipe one last time against my pebble-hard nipples before sliding down to my hips, taking ownership of me, now that I'm completely naked beneath him.

His tongue finds the tiny nub that aches for attention as he parts my legs and plants my feet on his shoulders.

Ohhh my...

I might have said it out loud. I'm really not sure. The only thing I'm sure of is that his mouth on me is almost maddening. Passion and heat pour from me, and he tastes me with his tongue, sliding downward to my slit and then upward again.

It's as close to an out of body experience as I'll ever have, almost as though I'm watching myself come against his mouth, so hard that it feels as though my body won't even survive it. His fingers dip into me as I throb and buck, even while his tongue on my clit seems to coax me along higher.

It's like skydiving, I'd imagine. Falling toward the ground but then whipped upward again from a sudden gust of wind that reminds you how powerless you really are.

That's exactly how it feels. Lacking any control for once in my life, Dodger Sheridan is that gust of wind that renders me powerless and I give into it, trusting him completely.

When the last vibration of my orgasm ripples through me, his eyes look up to mine.

"Are you sure this is what you want?" There's urgency and raw need flashing in his hot gaze on me. And it makes me want him even more, knowing he'd ask that right now, giving me the option to rethink this entire situation.

But rethinking anything is definitely not in the cards for me tonight.

"Yes, Dodger. Right now," I grind out the words, hoping that the part of him that remembers his years in the military will recognize an order when he hears it.

Yes, because this is the most alive I've ever felt and I don't want it to end with second thoughts or that damn practicality that seems to be my trademark.

Before tugging off his shorts and boxers completely, he pulls out a condom from the wallet he had in his pocket. And when I see his naked form, I'm almost stunned by it. He's a sight—ripped muscles formed in the Army and then maintained in an oceanfront weight room here in paradise, and a golden tan just the right tone to make his dark eyes seem even more intimidating.

Back home, I'd never even try for a man who looked like this. He's just not the type for a studious, hyper-focused lobbyist who pours her heart into a job that only found her dispensable when times were tough.

Yet here in Hawai'i, it seems too possible, too plausible, too tempting to resist. Even if this is nothing more than a dream that I'll awaken from on that long trek home to DC, I'm going to savor every moment of it.

When he sheaths himself with the condom, I open my

legs instinctively, sending a very clear message that the last thing I want right now is more foreplay.

I want *him*. Deep in me. Unrelenting.

Feeling the tip of him at my opening, he seems to hesitate for a split second and I'm fully prepared to cry—just wail and scream like a spoiled kid if I don't get my way. But, when he sees no hesitation from me, pure bliss overwhelms me when he plunges into me.

I gasp—perhaps from the size of him, but I think more from this unexpected sensation—this feeling of sudden completion, even though I'd never realized before that I was incomplete.

It's a dangerous feeling to have with a man who lives so far away from me. I recognize that, even with my brain soaked in passion; I know somehow that I'm playing with fire here. But I can't stop myself from doing it.

Striking against my innermost depths on the first thrust, I explode beneath him, the climax sudden and sweeping and consuming me completely. I've lost all sense of control, moaning as my channel seizes up around him again and again like I'm trying to take him in even deeper still.

He keeps his pace slow, easing in and out of me as my body recovers from release. "That's it, beautiful," he murmurs against my neck so tenderly, in stark contrast to the harsh desire that still has me in its grips.

Prickles of pleasure cascade over me as I descend down from the clouds of my climax. Feeling lightheaded, my heart pounds, yet I still want more—so much more of this feeling of wanton abandon. Each thrust gives me the pressure where I need it most, jarring against my depths and coaxing me upward again, already aching for another release.

Pressing my palms against his pecs, the thundering of his heartbeat echoes my own, reassuring me that his need is as strong and desperate as mine.

His hand eases my one leg higher up on his waist, and then he does the same with my other leg, angling me so that I'm even more vulnerable to his sweet invasion. He holds me like this, easing his cock in and out of me, watching me as he does—no doubt glorying in the power he has to make my eyelids flutter half-shut, to make my breasts rise and fall so quickly as I pant, to make my skin pebble up in goosebumps at the same time it sizzles with heat.

He seems to observe these things about me—my reactions, my emotions, my very soul somehow exposed—as though he's tucking away the knowledge for future use so that he'll bring me to even greater heights the next time he's takes me like this.

At least I *hope* that's why, because I want more of this. I want so much more it terrifies me because with less than a week left of my trip, I don't know how I'll possibly get enough to sustain me when I return home.

I can feel myself giving in to him, climbing upward on the spiral of desire with the only intention of propelling myself off when I can't take any more.

His voice coaxes me, whispering words to me that I seem to need to hear right now, with all that's going on in my life. I soak in the affirmations like a dry stretch of land that's finally saturated with a downpour.

Desire swelling in me again, I'm certain with each thrust that it will be his last. Yet his stamina is staggering.

Under the soft light coming from a nearby lamp, his body glistens, showcasing his muscles as they tighten with control, reigning in his desire.

Aching inside, my core coils up tightly, poised to explode.

I want to feel him shatter. I want the reassurance of it, needing desperately to know for a fact that this is bringing him the same level of abandon that it brings me.

"Now, Dodger. Please."

It's not lost to me how much I sound like I'm begging. Yet there's no shame in it. Only a need fueled by a fire he continues to stoke.

Until finally, he gives me what I desperately want, and I feel him shatter just as I arch and scream out his name. My own climax rips through me, rocking my entire body again and again, until my soul finally seems to sink back down into my conscious self.

He stays inside me as my channel quivers with aftershocks. With my eyes still shut, breath heaving, I feel his lips consume mine just before he leaves my body.

"Stay the night." His words somehow comfort me, because it would kill me to leave him now and go back to Annie's.

I will stay the night. I seem to have no choice, because rationality doesn't seem to exist here in paradise.

I feel as though I've imprinted on him somehow, and I know that should terrify me. I know it because there's nothing practical about it and it won't last.

But at this moment, I'll find joy in the words he's saying to me, assuring me I can stay in his arms until the dawn.

Because right now, it's only him and me. Nothing else exists.

Nothing else matters.

CHAPTER 13

- DODGER -

It's just before dawn when my eyes open, creature of habit that I am. To my brain, apparently it matters very little that I spent half the night enjoying some of the best sex ever. I still wake up in time to see the first rays of sunlight touch our side of the island.

But this time, I'm not yet anxious to sit on my lanai with my coffee to welcome a new day. I much prefer just taking in the sight of Samantha as she slumbers next to me.

I've really done it this time.

It seemed like a perfectly fine arrangement last night, so perfect that I couldn't possibly do anything but act on it. Once... and then a couple times to follow. She's single— thank God because when she showed up on my doorstep last night, I was ready to end the night exactly the way we did, Carl or not.

And I don't need to remind myself that *I'm* single.

So this should be perfect.

Except that she's leaving soon. *And* she's one of my sister-in-law's best friends, godmother to my niece.

That means I'll likely have to see her again from time to time, each time Annie kindly pops out another niece or nephew for me to spoil rotten. So when either or both of us has paired off with someone else, won't that be awkward?

I could probably handle that, I consider. Then I glance at her again, her eyes fluttering as though she's lost in a dream, and I feel this warmth inside of me that doesn't mesh up with the brief span of time she's been here. It's too early for this—these feelings that I can't deny are stirring inside me.

I can't even blame the post-sex haze for clouding my judgement. Because the fact is, I've felt this connection with her for days now, even though there's nothing logical about it.

Frowning, I'm reminded of what my brothers always tell me. *Dodger, you think too damn much.*

Stirring beneath a sheet that only half covers her gorgeous body, Samantha lets out a languid sigh as her eyes open.

Damn, I thought tropical sunrises were the best way to greet the morning. They pale in comparison to this.

"Hey," she breathes out contentedly.

"Good morning. Want me to get you some coffee?" I like that I already know how she likes it. I like that having her here with me almost seems like a routine.

A routine I could definitely get used to.

"Not yet. I love listening to the ocean in the morning."

"Me, too."

"Sooo..." she finally begins, as though it's a word that needs to be said. "That was nice."

"Nice. That's a pretty conservative statement," I notice. "I would have gone for a bit stronger language than that."

She laughs. "So you're a doctor *and* an editor this morning?"

"If I really was an editor, I wouldn't edit out a damn thing from last night," I can't help pointing out. "Except I might have just extended the whole thing. Make the night stretch a lot longer." Make your time here stretch a lot longer, too, I add in my head.

She climbs on top of me, and I feel myself respond immediately to the feel of her warmth against me. "That's what the morning's for," she says and kisses me deeply.

I immediately harden when her tongue slips inside me. Just like last night, any semblance of brain activity seems to be muted by sheer desire. My cock brushes against her as she straddles me, and I can already feel moisture in her channel. And just knowing how much she wants this is like tossing lighter fluid on the fire that burns in me.

Not good.

Not good at all, when it's so damn easy for me to slide into her. Too easy to succumb to stupidity and just feel her with nothing between us. Just spill myself into her and feel the glory of taking her like that.

I'd love it too much.

Still straddling me as I grow harder by the instant, she lowers her mouth to mine, her tongue teasing me the same way my cock is teasing her. She seems to say *yes* with her body; her eyes are almost hazy, hopefully as drunk on lust as I am right now.

But I can't take advantage of her like that.

So I reach for a condom from my nightstand. She pulls it from my hand and there's a split second that I'm hoping she'll toss it onto the floor. But instead, she tears it open with her teeth—a sight that makes me smile—and slides it onto me.

I like it this way, I decide as she lowers her sweet body

onto my length. I like that I simply don't have a choice in the matter right now. With her in control, I can shrug my shoulders at the tiny voices in my head that seem to be louder after the sun rises.

I can just savor her as she slides up and down me, the slickness and heat making me moan with pleasure. She's a hell of a sight—her skin so soft and curves that make her look so real and tempting. There's nothing manufactured about her, and I love that. I see enough tourists on this island, showcasing their beach-ready bodies that they practically picked out of a catalog at the plastic surgeon's office. I prefer a woman like this.

I grip those soft hips of hers and pull her down onto me so that the tip of my cock is hard at her womb and she can feel me throb inside her completely. Arching upward then, I move my hips so that I'm pressing against her clit with the root of me, and she grinds against me, seeking satisfaction.

Her eyes are shut, chasing pleasure, and I glory in the sight of it. There's nothing better than watching a woman come, and with this woman, it's even more gratifying for some unknown reason. It's as though bringing her this level of satisfaction is somehow what I was born to do.

Her lips part slightly and I hear a whimper pass through them. Breath quickening, her channel tightens up around me and I feel a smile on my lips, knowing the show I'm about to enjoy. Back arching, her breasts heave above me, nipples hard and aching for my touch. So I heed the call, moving my hands to her, massaging her even as I throb inside her.

Unrelenting passion builds in her; I can see it even with her eyes shut—and I can feel it, the way she grows so tight around me. It's all I can do to hold myself back when she cries out, hips bucking on sheer instinct and channel seizing me in glorious fits and starts. Her climax consumes her—and I revel in the sight of it. Still holding myself back, all my senses savor the way it feels and looks and sounds knowing that I'm possessing her—and feeling in my gut that no man has ever taken her quite as completely as I have.

After her last shudder and she sinks onto me, I roll her over, letting the cool sheets touch her back with me still rock-hard inside of her. I know she needs time to recover, and I give her that, taking her slowly even though it pains me to do so.

The sun creeps past my blinds and strikes us, my only reminder that time really is passing here in our tiny pocket of paradise. Yet still, I keep my pace unhurried, savoring the slide of me inside her. My hands grip her wrists—not in domination—at least I tell myself it's not. But the hold I have on her lets me feel her pulse slowly return to normal again as she recovers from the climax.

Her eyes finally open, as though she's coming out of a dream. I kiss her, long and hard, letting my tongue enjoy the taste of her, until the pads of my thumbs at her wrists feel her heart rate quicken again.

It's my turn now, I can't help thinking. I need to find that same satisfaction that she did. I need to own her with my body. My thrusts quicken and fire flashes again in her.

I watch each breath fill her lungs bringing her breasts closer to me. When I'm deep in her, I take an extra moment to press against her where she needs it the most, coaxing her toward another climax, because I'm convinced there's nothing—*nothing*—that is more satisfying than coming together as we did so many times last night.

I feel as if I've memorized her body, her reactions, her every button that I can push to make her heart race even more. Yet just when I'm confident that there's nothing left to learn, I find a new way to rouse her upward.

It's like there's an endless discovery with her—and one I'm not going to take lightly.

Finally, when I know she's poised to explode, I give in to my need and shatter with her.

Our breath is in perfect unison, and I'm satisfied beyond belief. I could lay like this forever, holding her, until a pesky ray of sunlight through my shades finds her eyes and she squints.

"Another sunny day on the Kona side of the island," she says as though the statement has some significance to her.

My eyebrows rise in question.

"It's what Annie always said in her texts back when I was in DC," she explains.

"A truer statement was never said."

"You've got the sun, the great Kona coffee. What else does this island offer?"

"After what we just did, I should be insulted that you'd even need to ask." I force myself to get up and toss the condom in the trash. Standing now, with just enough space between us, I feel a new need overcome me. "Speaking of Kona coffee, there's a mug with my name on it about this time." As much as I love the idea of lying here all day with her, there's no need to scare her away when my java addiction bares its teeth. "Care to join me?"

Slowly rising, she gives her head a soft shake, almost in disbelief. "There's something about Hawai'i that always makes me want to get up and greet the day outside. I don't know if I'd ever sleep in if I lived here."

I smile at the notion that she likes it here. Then I scold myself for daring to think she might like it enough to stay.

Downstairs, we eat some fruit out on the lanai and I watch how she gazes out to the ocean as though it will somehow provide all the answers to life's questions. I can relate to that.

"I'm sorry about Carl," I find myself saying. I hate to bring it up for fear it might destroy this perfection we've been enjoying. But she was with the guy for a long time.

Wordless, she glances over at me.

"Well, not *really* sorry because I never actually liked the guy," I confess. Even if he wasn't a phone addict, I hated the way he wouldn't wear his lei of kukui nuts at Cam and Annie's wedding. Who refuses a lei in Hawai'i? "But I know you were together for more than a minute."

She shrugs. "Losing him wasn't nearly as hard as losing my job."

My brow creases sharply. "Your *job?*"

"Yeah. I got laid off a few weeks ago."

"Oh, God, Samantha. You've really been through it. Why didn't you tell me?"

She angles a look at me. "If I couldn't bring myself to share it with Annie..." Her voice trails as she releases a sigh.

"You don't like to share your burdens, do you?"

Her body almost shivers at the notion for a brief moment, as if the idea is offensive to her. "It just doesn't come naturally to me, no."

"Why not?"

"Just the way I am, I guess." She gives a dismissive shrug.

I reach over and gently take her hand in mine. And just like every other time I touch her, the sensation stuns me. "I'm sorry about your job. I can imagine how much it must hurt because you loved it so much."

"It's all right," she tells me, looking away, like she might fall apart right now if our eyes met. "I'm hoping this will lead to something better."

"Things often happen that way," I agree.

"Right. Exactly," she states, seeming to reassure herself. "I was at the top of my game when they laid me off. So I've already had lots of interviews. I even got a few second interviews from some organizations where I have contacts."

"No firms this time?" I ask, remembering our conversation from before.

She bobbles her head a little. "I thought, so long as I have to look for a job, I might as well first try for something that I'll love even more. So I reached out to some causes I really believe in—like cancer research because my uncle died of it recently, and one organization that fights for more affordable child care options because my mom really struggled with that when I was a kid. A couple environmental organizations. Things like that."

"It would be great to pour all that passion you have for lobbying into a mission you really care about," I concur.

"That's what I figured." She takes a sip of her coffee, looking optimistic for a moment until the look fades. "But as you know, my phone is undeniably silent. Well, except for a rejection email here and there."

"It takes time to find the right thing," I remind her.

"Yeah. I might have to apply to some firms next. You know, if I don't hear anything before I go home."

Only when I see the empty look on her face just now does it settle in. "So you lost your job and he left you?" I shake my head, disbelieving. "If I disliked the guy before, I'm hating him now." I can't help it when I feel my fists ball up instinctively. He's lucky there's an ocean and a continent in between us.

"That's not exactly accurate either. He left me *because* I lost my job."

"*What?*"

"He liked being my date when I went to the galas and events and social things that I was required to attend for the firm. He liked getting his picture taken with the President and senators and powerful people. Honestly, his damn office is covered in them." She lets out a brief laugh. "I think *he* was more upset I lost my job than *I* was."

"What a shitbag," I can't prevent from slipping out.

She laughs. "You don't sound much like a doctor when you say things like that."

"Yeah, well, I'm not wearing my white coat right now," I grumble.

"The way it happened, it almost made it easier. How can I miss a guy when he'd leave when things are at their worst?" She gives a dismissive wave. "But he was good to me when we were together. He never swept me off my feet, but it all seemed to fit. It was… I don't know…"

"Logical?" I offer, thinking immediately about Hailey.

"Yeah. When I think about it, yeah. But it sounds terrible to say that out loud, though. Logical and… practical."

"I can't throw any stones. I was in the same type of relationship."

"At least she didn't dump you for getting fired. I mean, when it happened, I didn't expect Carl to show up with a sparkling ring on the Capitol steps one evening and profess his undying love. I never thought of myself as someone who needed that sort of thing—you know, grand gestures and riding off into the sunset on a white horse or whatever," she finishes sounding rather deflated.

I nod. "Maybe. But when you go through something like losing a job, you were due for a reminder that there might be a silver lining," I theorize, having what my mother used to call a *learning moment* back when I was a kid. Because truth is, I can't say I've ever swept a girl off her feet either. I've planned some pretty romantic evenings; it's easy to do on this island. Yet there were no white horses involved, or anything worthy of a chick flick or those TV movies Annie watches over the holidays.

"Yeah. After two years together, I sure didn't expect to get dumped," she mutters in response.

The irony hits me. "You got dumped for getting fired.

And Hailey dumped me for getting *hired*." I shift uneasily in my seat. "I don't like to admit it, but it was a bit of a blow to my ego to think that a new job at the Grand Canyon had more appeal to her than I did."

Amusement in her eyes, she tilts her head. "The Grand Canyon *is* pretty spectacular. Although after last night, I think Hailey needs her brain checked."

I chuckle, grateful for the confidence boost from her. "It was a new challenge for her. She'd seen and done it all here. Learned all she could. She was ready to move on."

She nods. "Annie said you have a tendency to fall for women who leave."

Her words strike me somehow, because until now, I'd have said I don't *fall* for anyone. Falling for someone implies a sense of helplessness, as though a person has been tossed off the edge of a cliff and lost all sense of control.

I never felt that sensation with Hailey. Until right now, I'd have thought my rational brain would have disallowed such a thing.

Until right now as I touch Samantha... which makes no sense at all after only a short time with her.

"I guess she's right," I reply, squeezing her hand slightly before forcing myself to let go.

Falling. That's just how this feels.

Shit. This is not good.

"Well, if it makes you feel better," she begins, "after last night I can say that you could have any woman on the island. You've got some mad skills."

"I'll take that compliment," I say, realizing that I don't *want* any other woman on the island. I just want her. "And I'll tell *you* that you can definitely do better than Carl. In fact—" I lean in to take a taste of her. "—I'd like to think you just did."

"God, yes," she purrs as she moves to my lips.

I can taste the cream and sugar from her coffee on her breath, or maybe that's just her natural essence. I could be easily convinced of that.

"About this whole notion of you staying with Annie and Cam…" I dare to begin when our lips part.

Her eyes meet mine. My pecs tighten, almost like my heart is about to escape my ribcage and I'm trying to hold fast to it. Just looking at her has that effect on me.

"Yes?" she prods when I pause a little too long.

"I know you want to spend some time with Annie and the baby, but I'm kind of hoping that I might be able to convince you to spend your nights here. I've got the next couple days off now so…"

She nods stoically. "So you might get lonely?"

A half smile slides upward on my face. "Yeah."

"Well, I wouldn't want that. Not after you've been so nice to me."

Pulling her onto my lap, I grin. Her gentle weight on me makes all my blood surge south and I grow harder by the second. "You didn't take much convincing," I note.

Angling her head, her lips so tempting, she glances downward, probably at the feel of just how much I want her.

She grins. "Apparently, neither did you."

CHAPTER 14

~ SAMANTHA ~

Twice before nine. I ponder that thought with a silly grin pasted on my face as I watch Dodger's impressive backside disappear into the bathroom for a shower. And while he invited me to join him, I'm finding I need to catch my breath.

I'm trying to remember the last time I had sex twice before nine in the morning.

Nope, just can't do it.

This could be addictive, I realize as I finally pick up my phone for the first time this morning. Funny how being with Dodger tamps down the impulse to constantly check my phone for news on the job-hunting front.

Besides, I owe Annie a text.

"Hey. Sorry I bolted last night," I write.

Annie's reply is immediate. "I've been waiting for this text all morning! WTF?"

I pause, wondering what the *WTF* was for exactly. Was it

because I so rudely left after dinner? Or was it for the fact that I darted over here the moment I found out Dodger was oh-so-available?

I'm betting it's the latter. And if there was any question, I can clarify right now because my phone rings and Annie's photo pops up on my display.

"That didn't take you long," I tease.

"Did you just hook up with my brother-in-law?" she blurts.

I blush from head to toe as though her words have me reliving the last ten hours of my life. "Maybe."

"Oh my God. I never predicted this, Sam. I mean, you guys barely talked at the wedding or baptism. And I thought you were still with that bastard."

I laugh at how quickly my friend has lost the ability to utter Carl's name. From henceforward, I predict he will always be referred to as some expletive or another.

"Do I have to remind you again that you've got a baby on the brink of talking?" I scold at the sound of her language.

"Oh, she's out with Cam right now. Which is good because I need a little space to let all this sink in. First, you tell me you got laid off. Then about Carl who, by the way, I never liked anyway."

"Apparently, you're not alone in that opinion."

"And now I'm learning that you and Dodger hooked up. I know things move at a faster pace where you're from. But this is crazy. So what happened? No wait—I don't need details. He *is* my brother-in-law."

"Well, I guess it's safe to say we had a nice night," I offer simply. Then grinning, I can't help adding, "and morning."

"Oh my..." she breathes out. "And you're leaving next week. I don't foresee a happy ending to this."

My shoulders droop. "No. I guess not. But he's been teaching me a thing or two about shutting my laptop, setting down my phone, and just enjoying the moment. So I'm not going to think about that right now."

"Sounds like a plan," she says uncertainly. "So does this mean staying with Cam and me has lost its appeal?"

Feeling like the worst kind of friend, I cringe. "Would you mind? I still want to spend lots of time with you and the baby, but…"

"You don't have to say another word. Frankly, I was surprised you even wanted to come stay here at all after staying at Dodger's for a few nights. I mean, that view over there is incredible. And over here, let's face it, it's a lot of dirty diapers and baby toys," she finishes with a laugh.

"I love your place. It's just perfect for your family."

"Yeah, it's a good life," she says contentedly. I can hear the smile in her voice as she says it. But there's also a hint of relief in her tone, and only then do I realize just how much it takes out of her when her baby is sick.

Parenting is a terrifying expedition, I decide.

"So, do you want to do something today?" I ask her, hearing the shower turn off in Dodger's bathroom and feeling a little shiver from the idea of him in there— naked, hot, and wet. It's a picture I shouldn't be drawing up in my head while talking to my friend.

"I'm actually taking Baby K in to her new pediatrician," she answers.

"Oh no. Is she sick again?"

"No. She's great. It's just for follow-up. So unless he's working, I'm betting Dodger can come up with some better way to entertain you today."

I grin. "He said he's got the next couple days off."

"Then how about we all meet at the beach for a picnic tonight if the pediatrician says Baby K's ready for it?"

"That sounds perfect."

"In the meantime, just have some fun with Dodger. You

need this. Hell, after what you've been through, you *deserve* this. He'll show you a better time than we could." She bursts out laughing. "But you apparently already figured that out."

She's still laughing when I hang up the phone a few minutes later.

My cheeks puff out as I set down my phone. I'm somehow on edge after the conversation. Annie's right—I'm leaving. And while having a fling with this man seems fun right now, it won't be fun when I have to face him years from now when I visit Annie and he shows up with some new woman on his arm.

God, that's going to suck.

How could I have been this stupid?

And then, as if on cue, he steps out of his bathroom clad in nothing but a towel.

A skimpy towel at that.

That's how I could have been this stupid. Looking at him makes me fifty shades of stupid every time.

Silently, I soak in the sight of him.

Holy crap.

I don't even realize that I shared that sentiment out loud till he cocks his head and grins.

"I'm hoping you meant that in a positive way," he says.

I don't even dignify that with an answer. How else could I possibly mean it?

"What do you *do* to look like that, Dodger?" I can't resist ogling him for a moment, especially since he doesn't seem to mind. Most men as tall as Dodger tend to be lankier. Even if they're in great shape, they usually have the build of something like a marathon runner. But Dodger's thick, corded muscles look like something sketched by Michelangelo—the epitome of the male form.

And I get to touch him.

Seriously, I'm feeling so lucky I might pick up a few lottery tickets later today.

He laughs, sitting alongside me on the bed. "So, what would you like to do today?"

The way I'm looking at him, I can't imagine he even needs to ask. I force my eyes to meet his. "You're still up for spending the day with me?" I ask, somehow needing the reassurance.

"Of course. Why wouldn't I be?"

I shrug. "Oh, I don't know. I'm not that experienced when it comes to flings, but a lot of guys... well, they reach this point and they're kind of happy to move on to something new."

He nudges me onto my back. "First off, I'm not most guys."

"I can tell that just by looking at you," I can't help noting.

"And secondly, I *am* ready for something new. Like maybe in the shower next time. It was pretty lonely in there." He blankets my body with his own and I can feel the hard ridge of him through the towel. His mouth dips to mine and he tastes fresh and minty and thoroughly desirable. "Now about today," he continues. "There's plenty we still have left to see and do on the island."

I giggle when his hand traces along the fabric of the nightshirt I'm wearing and then cups my breast, the light touch tickling me. "Snorkeling, lava, and stargazing are going to be hard to top," I tell him.

"Mmhm. You know what we could do?" He lifts my shirt and sucks in my nipple.

I whimper low and desperate before I can even reply, "I'm hoping I can guess."

"Boogie boarding."

My head lifts off the pillow to eye him. "That's not what I was thinking."

"I'd take you surfing, but I suck at it. I can show you how to boogie board though. Even though I'm not very good at that, either."

"Dodger, even *kids* can boogie board," I tease, having spent some time on the Jersey shore as a child.

"Yeah, but I'm six-four. Have you ever seen a guy my size trying to fit on a boogie board? It's almost as pathetic as me surfing."

"It's a wonder you stick around this island." I slide my hands downward along his back and am rewarded by his moan when I reach the towel at his waist. Our lips meet again, a slow, tentative tangle of our tongues.

"Annie suggested we meet up for a picnic dinner tonight," I say when we come up for air. "But in the meantime, I think I'd like to see that green sand you mentioned the other day. Everyone talks about it," I suggest. Even though the idea of just staying in bed with him all day is appealing, I can't deny I'll be stressing over my job hunt. And if I'm this close to my laptop, I'll be reminded of what I really should be doing right now.

"Perfect. We'll drive down to Papakolea today, and then maybe tomorrow I'll take you to Punaluʻu."

"What's that?"

"My favorite black sand beach. You can usually see endangered sea turtles there, too."

"Oh, that sounds nice."

He grins, his lips still against my skin with kisses tracking lower to my belly.

"But first—" He reaches my panties and starts to pull them downward.

I inhale sharply at the feel of his breath on me where I desperately want to be touched. "First what?"

"First, there's one other activity you might like on this island."

"Oh, really. And what's that?"

He raises an eyebrow. "If you really don't know, then I guess I'll have to show you," he murmurs as he slides my panties off and takes me with his mouth.

Slipping into a state of ecstasy, my head lolls to the side as his tongue and fingers toy with me. I can't help noticing the clock that stares at me from his nightstand.

Three times before nine, I amend my prior observation.

I could get used to this.

CHAPTER 15

- DODGER –

Stretching my legs out in front of me, I sit at a small café table a few doors down from my clinic, staring out at Mauna Lani Drive just after daybreak. It's been my routine to start my work week here with my brother. Usually, I like our little tradition.

Yet this morning, after two glorious days showing off the island to Samantha, this coffee tastes like a bitter reminder that I have to spend the next eight hours away from her.

"So what do you think?" Cam's voice snaps me back to reality.

And just like that, I realize that I need to get another coffee before starting my morning shift.

Either that, or I need to get my head out of my ass.

I look over at him, trying to remember what we were talking about.

"I think that's great," I say absentmindedly. Knowing

Cam, it either has to do with some plans for expanding his website or whether he should start buying the next size up clothing for his baby to allow for growing room.

Cam's eyes narrow on me. "Good. So, know any good divorce lawyers?"

"What?" I screw my face up.

"Dude, I just told you that I was leaving my wife for an underwear model." He folds his arms across his chest. "You haven't heard a damn thing I've said all morning. Where the hell are you today?"

"Sorry, man."

"Get your mind in the game, Son," he says in that tone we all use to mimic every Army commander we've had… well, *ever.*

"I said I was sorry. I didn't sleep much last night. So I assume you don't need a lawyer?"

"Nope." He takes a loud sip of his coffee. "Just some new onesies. I think that cold she had somehow made Baby K grow an entire size overnight. Does that happen?"

"Uh, no. Not from colds. Babies just grow, Bro." I frown at how typical conversations have gotten with my Ranger brother. It seems like just yesterday when every discussion we had was focused on some new adventure we were planning. Now, he's obsessing over onesies.

Why do I envy him right now?

"So did you like that new pediatrician I found you?" I ask.

"Yep. A lot more than the last guy. We already have our next well-baby appointment scheduled with her." He throws back a gulp of coffee as though he's a college kid doing shots. "It's about fifteen minutes further away from us but it'll be nice to go to a clinic that always has an on-call doctor who actually returns calls."

"Yeah, imagine that."

Tilting his head, he narrows his eyes on me. "Where's

your head these days, Dodger? You're used to the lack of sleep. So it can't be that."

"My head's right here on top of my shoulders." My tone is defensive. I'm tired; that's all it is. The last two days we hit the green sand at Papakolea, black sand at Punalu'u, and petroglyphs at Puako. And whenever we weren't hiking or driving, our bodies were entangled in ways that would challenge the most limber yoga instructor on the island. "Might be that you've just got nothing halfway interesting to talk about anymore."

A sly grin slides up one of his cheeks. "You're full of shit, Dodger. You're thinking about Sam. About how she's leaving so soon."

"Am not."

"Are too," he says, and before I open my mouth to reply, I cut myself short because, as his brother, I know we'll keep repeating the same words to each other at least six times like we did when we were kids. *Am not... are too... am not...* usually only stopping when my mother threatened to ground us if we didn't shut up.

"Look," I say instead, "I know she's leaving. I'm not an idiot. I'm not thinking there's anything else between us other than just a nice fling."

"Nah. You're enjoying her too much to think of this as just a fling. I mean, come on, it's got to be refreshing compared to the girls you've been dating lately."

"There's nothing wrong with the women I date."

He angles a look at me. "Nothing wrong with *them*. But plenty wrong with *you* for thinking they might be a good match for you in the first place. Like that girl Annie and I met when we bumped into you at the Dancing Coconut a couple weeks ago." He shakes his head. "If you rubbed the two digits of her IQ together, you could build a fire."

I'm just tired enough that it takes me several beats to even figure out what he means by that. "You don't have to be insulting, Cam," I grumble, sounding way too much like my dad when I do.

"Maybe I do to make my point. Since Hailey left, you keep dating these women whose greatest ambition is to not break a nail while they're posting on Instagram. Because you can't handle having a woman who might have any kind of ambition."

My back straightens. "Cam, here's the fact: if a woman has any kind of ambition, there's a high probability she's not going to be sticking around the island. Look at my track record."

"Like Sam."

I sigh. "Yeah. Like Samantha. I'm having a fling with her. No big deal. She's leaving and I'm happy that she has a life she loves elsewhere." I practically bark the words. "I'm not letting my feelings get wrapped up in another woman who's just going to leave like Hailey did," I say, even though I know it's too late for me there. *Feelings* seem to be the *only* thing stirring inside of me when I think of Samantha. No logic. Just feelings that are driven by instinct.

Cam makes one of those childish *psht* noises, slicing his hand through the air. "You never loved Hailey."

"We were together a long time, Cam. Of course I loved her."

"You didn't. Not really. Or you'd still be with her."

I glare. "She got a job elsewhere. And my job is here."

"Dodger, when you love someone, you make it work. Look at Fen and Kaila. They were thousands of miles apart for most of their relationship until they got engaged. But they found a way to make it work."

"That's an exception."

"Then I guess I'm an exception too because you know if Annie had needed to go back to DC after that work crap cleared up for her, I would have followed her. I would have swum across the damn ocean to get to her if that was the only way. That's what love is. And you no more loved Hailey in *that* way than any of us did. She was a great girl. But you can't tell me she was your soulmate."

"Soulmate," I scoff at the word. "What the hell happened to my little brother?"

"*Love* did, man," he says in a tone that makes me think we're in a crowded congregation and he's testifying that his soul was saved. "And I know you think you're supposed to know everything just because you're the oldest. But I'm here to tell you that when it hits you, when it's right, you're not going to let miles or anything else come between you."

I hate the idea of him being right.

I hate it, until eight hours later when I walk through my condo door and see Samantha waiting for me on the lanai.

Because when I look at her now, I feel like my soul was just saved, too.

CHAPTER 16

~ SAMANTHA ~

It seems too natural, too right sometimes with Dodger. Like right now, stretched out on his bed. One of my ears is pressed against his chest, listening to the gentle beat of his heart, and the other can hear the ocean waves right outside the door to his upstairs lanai.

I'm not sure which sound is more relaxing to me. But together, they make me feel like a different person.

"Another sunny day on the Kona side of the island," he murmurs to me, repeating the words I'd said to him once, and sliding his fingers through my hair. Then he shifts slightly and I feel his lips press against the top of my head.

I know this is just temporary. But I also know that every relationship I ever have in the future will be measured against this... perfection. For the rest of my life, I'll be comparing men to Dodger.

Yet it's even more complex than that. It's as though I

know I'll be comparing this way I feel in Dodger's arms to every sensation I experience in my life. Do I feel as safe as I felt with Dodger? As nurtured? As fulfilled? I can hear the questions I'll ask myself in the future, and I fear the answer will always be *no*.

I've never been the biggest fan of the concept of love. It took me six months to even utter the word to Carl, doing so only at that point where I thought our relationship must progress because our lives seemed to meld together well, both our paths headed in the same direction.

Looking back, I see that while we might have been headed to the same destination, we were still on distinctly separate paths.

Yet even knowing this, I find myself clinging to the idea that there has to be some practical component to love—something grounded in mutual goals or a long track record of shared experiences. Neither of which I share with Dodger.

Or geography. Yeah, it should be essential that two people in love at least share the same geography.

Also unlike Dodger and me.

But love or not, this feeling I have with him is nothing short of addictive.

I sigh contentedly, feeling unable to speak just yet.

"I hate that I have to work tonight," he says, his tone filled with regret.

I find myself sighing yet again, not liking the idea of watching a sunset tonight without him. Even worse, I can't help wondering what it will feel like on the other side of the planet watching the day end and knowing he's so far away.

And why am I even *thinking* things like this after such a short time together?

"At least we have today," I point out optimistically. "What do you want to do today?"

"I'm game for anything. I can take you over to Hilo;

they've got some great restaurants. Or, we can hit those farm tours you said you were interested in. You know—coffee beans and stuff."

Flopping onto my back and watching the ceiling fan above me spin hypnotically, I think back to all the things I've seen on this island. The sand in so many different colors, the waters of every shade of blue imaginable, the marine wildlife that I never thought I'd see, living my DC life on the banks of the Potomac River.

Yet still, there's one thing I'd love to accomplish while I'm here.

Taking a breath, I dare to say it. "I think I'd rather just sit tight here."

He shifts so that I can see his eyebrows rise. "You're not planning on spending this gorgeous day staring at job listings on your laptop, are you?"

"I should. I really should. But—" I catch myself pausing, almost trying to force myself to say what I should say... something like, *but I need to find a job. But I have bills to pay that will be waiting for me. But the longer I stay out of the lobbying game, the less likely I'll find a good job.*

Yet I don't say any of those things. "But I think I just want to relax today."

"Relax?" His eyes narrowing, he pulls away from me slightly. "Who are you, and what did you do with the Samantha I know?"

I laugh. "Yeah, I'm starting to wonder that myself, actually," I admit.

"Samantha... relaxing," he says thoughtfully. "I'm going to have to take a picture of this because I bet Annie won't believe it."

I giggle as he slides his hand upwards along my belly until he cups my face in his hand and kisses me so gently that I sigh *again* this morning, even though I must sound like a love-struck teen.

"So, this relaxation thing you seem to enjoy…" I begin. "I'm hoping there will be a margarita on the beach involved."

He grins. "That can be arranged."

"And I'll need your help with the sunscreen, of course," I add, remembering the feel of his hands on my back that day on the boat.

"I think I can help you there."

"Good." I stretch out like a cat. "I think I'm liking the idea of relaxing. I just hope I don't get too addicted to it. Doesn't quite meld with my life back home."

"There are places to relax in DC."

If I had any desire to move right now, I'd probably raise an eyebrow at his words. "Dodger, you know what it's like back there."

"I do."

"And did *you* actually find time to relax when you lived there?" My tone is accusatory.

His lips form a frown. "No, I didn't. But that was just the job I was in. Looking back, I should have done some things differently."

"Like what?"

"Like gone hiking at Great Falls. I always wanted to do that. But just never got the time for it. Or gone biking on the Capital Crescent Trail. Or seen more of the museums."

My eyes widen. "Oh, I know. Tell me about it. After work, I'd always try to watch the sunset from the steps of the Capitol Building because my office was so close by. It's gorgeous, you know. The skies turn pink and orange at that time of day and the Washington Monument and all the memorials reflect the colors. It's almost magical." I pause for a moment, lost in the memory of it, feeling that familiar surge of being a part of a city that holds so much power and promise. And for the first time since I got here, I almost miss it, even here in Dodger's arms.

I *almost* look forward to being home.

Until I remember I have no job there, no purpose, no all-important title or stack of business cards. I frown at the thought.

"Sunset at the Capitol Building," he whispers lowering a kiss to the top of my head as I rest my cheek against his chest again. "That sounds like a good way to end a day."

I nod against him. "It is. But I'd sit there for those ten minutes or so, and I'd look at all those beautiful Smithsonian museums lined up along the Mall and wonder when I'd have a full day free to actually explore one or two of them."

"You never went to *any* of them?"

I think for a moment. "Well, I had a lunch meeting once at the National Museum of the American Indian. Does that count?"

"In your case, it might have to," he grumbles.

"I admire you, Dodger," I admit, knowing that saying so only exemplifies my own failings. But I don't mind being flawed around him. "You balance work with fun. You go to your clinic for eight hours, but then when you walk away, you have so many things you do that have nothing at all to do with being a doctor or advancing your career. I want to try to be a little more like that when I get back."

I hear him chuckle against my cheek.

"Don't laugh at me," I scold, giving his abs a light smack and then regretting it because it's a little like slapping a slab of concrete.

"I'm not laughing at you. I was actually thinking that I wish I was a little bit more like you."

I expel a skeptical snort. "What is it you admire? Is it the way I pop Tums through my work day like they're breath mints, or the fact that I should probably walk around with a blood pressure cuff attached to me?"

"No. Definitely neither of those. But you love your career. I can see it in your eyes. You light up when you talk about making an impact on the world."

I scoff. "A meteor makes an impact. I don't."

"You know that's not true."

I lift my head to look at him, resting my chin on his chest. "If I made such an impact, you'd think my phone would be ringing with job offers." At that, I can't resist rolling off him and reaching for my phone just to confirm that, *no*, there are still no voicemails or messages from potential employers. Just a forwarded news article from my mom about one of my former clients and one text from Annie, reminding me that they're picking me up for dinner at the Dancing Coconut tonight after Dodger leaves for work.

"It's only been a few weeks," he reminds me, gently taking my phone from my grasp and setting it back on his night-stand. "So, where do you want to relax today?" he says, bless-edly changing the subject.

"Where would you suggest?"

"Well, if it was my choice, we'd stay right here in bed."

"I could be swayed to do that," I admit.

"Nah. You said sunscreen should be involved. So I'm thinking maybe right out at Mauna Kea Beach. That way I'm a thirty-second walk to my kitchen so I can keep hooking you up with as many margarita refills as you need."

The smile on my lips seems etched so deeply that I'd swear it touches right down to my soul.

"I think that sounds perfect."

CHAPTER 17

- DODGER -

On weekdays like today, there's barely a soul here on the tranquil section of beachfront that lies adjacent to my condo. Samantha is stretched out on a towel with my baseball cap over her face. With its olive drab coloring and the 101st Airborne Division insignia on its front, I'd bet she was a military wife, maybe grabbing a weekend away from Schofield Barracks on O'ahu where her husband is stationed. Because now that she has a little color on her skin, she looks more like she fits in here.

I only wish that was the case.

"Hey," I say, dragging a couple chairs as I approach her. "Sit in one of these. You'll get some shade."

Lazily, she peeks out from beneath the cap and eyes me curiously as I open the chairs.

"Oh, that's ingenious," she says when she sees the built-in

shades along the tops of the chairs. "Where did you get those?"

"Target."

"You have a Target?"

"We're not *that* uncivilized here," I say with mock sarcasm. "Where do you think Annie gets diapers?"

She laughs. "I never thought about it. Diapers are generally not in the forefront of my brain."

Curious, I cock my head, grabbing her drink from the sand and sliding it into one of the chair's built-in cup holders. "Do you want kids one day?"

She gives a distinct nod. "Within the next five years."

My eyes widen, then squint again when a gust blows some sand our way. "You say that as though you've already marked off the time in your Outlook calendar."

Her eyes widen with innocence. "And what if I did? I'm from DC, you know. That's how we do things." Reaching for her drink, she grins at me, then lazily looks out to the ocean. "I've been thrown off a bit because I'll have to start a new job. There's usually a certain amount of time you have to work someplace before you qualify for the maximum maternity benefits. And then of course with Carl out of the picture, I'll have to find someone in the DC area who would make an adequate father. You know, stable job, just handsome enough to be attractive to me, good conversationalist, and low debt-to-income ratio."

I chuckle, not just because there's humor in her own voice as she says all this, but because she sounds exactly like how my brothers always depict me. "You've thought this through."

"I'm very practical. That's what Annie says, anyway."

"I can't throw any stones," I admit. "My approach to relationships has been kind of the same as yours, I'm guessing."

"Really?"

"My brothers are always telling me that I'm very logical. Used to call me Spock when we were younger."

"Spock?"

"Yeah. You know, the Vulcan on *Star Trek*. He was always using logic."

She shrugs. "*Star Trek* predates me."

"Well, me, too. But he's a cultural icon," I say almost defensively. Truth is, I never even minded the nickname as a kid.

"So why are you so logical all the time?"

"Growing up, I always loved science. I loved how it had an answer for every question that I could possibly imagine."

She raises a single eyebrow. "I don't know. When we looked at all those stars the other night, all I had were more questions."

"Just because we don't know the answers yet, doesn't mean that there's not a good scientific explanation out there, waiting to be discovered." I say it with certainty, even though deep inside of me, I'm still struggling to find an adequate explanation for why I feel so strongly about someone who's been in my life for a matter of days.

There must be one. I just haven't figured it out yet.

I give myself an internal shake at the conundrum. "So how'd you get so practical?"

"Comes from the way I was raised, I guess. At Christmas, I was the kid who got things like socks and underpants under the tree."

I think back to what she told me that day we went snorkeling about her mom struggling to raise a child on her own. For as much as my brothers and I complained that we weren't being raised like our wealthy cousins, we never got underpants from Santa Claus.

"That had to be hard."

"Oh no," she quickly corrects. "I don't want to give the

wrong impression. I had a great childhood. My mom was the best. *Is* the best," she quickly corrects, almost sounding like she needs to remind herself this. "I think because she was a single mom, we bonded even more. And it might have been socks under the tree, but that night, we'd be doing a sock puppet show or something. We did well with what we had."

"Are you still close with her?"

"Yeah. She's in New Jersey where I was born, so it's not that far of a drive from DC."

"Did you tell her about your job?" I feel compelled to ask even though it's not my business.

She frowns for a moment, as though I read her mind just then and she's not very happy about it. Uneasily, she takes a sip of her drink. "No. I just don't want her to worry. Being unemployed... that whole concept will just dredge up a lot of bad memories for her. She's so scared I'll end up struggling like she did."

My forehead creases. "Uh, don't you think she'll figure it out? I mean, she might call you at your office one day."

She shakes her head. "With as much traveling as I did for work, she always calls my cell."

I stay silent for a moment, considering just how messed up that situation really is. For as much friction as I had with my father, I certainly wouldn't have hesitated to tell him that I lost my job. But I keep my mouth shut, reminding myself that she's leaving soon. The intricacies of her family relationships shouldn't matter to me.

Yet they do. I can't deny that.

She turns, narrowing her eyes on my frown. "Oh, come on, Dodger. Don't judge me."

"I'm not judging you at all."

She reaches for her phone in the side pocket of the chair. "Look at this," she says, scrolling through a string of recent texts from her mother. "Every one of these is somehow related to my job. She asks about it constantly."

I furrow my brow at all the links. "What's with all the articles?"

"They each mention some client of the firm in the news. She's like... the most effective RSS feed out there."

"She obviously is proud of you."

"Well, yeah, but it's more than that. She thinks she's helping me. When I succeed at work, it makes her feel like she's succeeding, because all she ever really wanted was for me to be able to not have to live paycheck-to-paycheck. She's a good person, Dodger. The best. I just can't take that away from her—that feeling that she succeeded, you know? She asks for so little out of life." She shakes her head again and repeats, "I just can't take that away from her. And why should I need to? Because I *will* find a job. It's just a matter of time."

I frown, somehow understanding, yet still not liking it. "So, you didn't tell *me* you lost your job... or Annie or your mom. Who *did* you tell?"

"Carl," she says with a laugh. "And see how that turned out? Look, I'm more comfortable with things that way. When I cry, I cry alone."

I don't like the idea of her crying at all, actually. Especially alone. "I want you to make me a promise. Next time you're crying alone, no matter where you are, I want you to find me. Whether I'm in the next room, or on the other end of a phone call."

"I don't need that," she scoffs.

"Samantha, don't even get me started about how important mental health is," I say, using my doctor-tone that my brothers hate.

"A few tears here and there don't mean I have poor mental health."

"No, you're right. Tears are healthy. But feeling like you can't share them with someone who—" I stumble on my words, unwilling to admit to myself the pesky *L-word* nearly slipped past my lips because it's way too early for that. "—cares about you is not good." I touch her arm and feel that flash of awareness that I always do. And I see the irony of the situation. If I *hadn't* slept with her, I wouldn't hesitate to tell her that she's loved by me, and by my brother and sister-in-law. She's part of our family. Yet because we're having sex, the word seems to imply something else entirely if I let it slip.

Although just now, those implications don't seem too far off the mark. "Promise me right now," I finish when I see the reluctance in her eyes.

"Dodger, you're being ridiculous."

I pull the can from her drink holder. "Promise me or I'm pouring this out."

"You wouldn't," she glares at me over the tops of her sunglasses.

"Watch me," I threaten with a devilish grin, angling the can slightly.

"Okay, okay. I promise. You know, you play dirty, Dr. Sheridan." She snatches the drink from my extended hand and takes a hefty gulp.

I grin as she sets her drink down on the opposite side of her chair this time, out of my reach. "I guess I can tell you now that I've got another six-pack of those in the fridge."

She fires me a look of admonishment. "You are such a child."

"My brothers are much worse. Ask Annie."

"Yeah, she's mentioned something about that." She reaches for her drink again and gives it a long, appreciative look. "I can't believe I had to come all the way to Hawai'i to discover there's such a thing as a margarita in a can."

"I know. The stores around here carry all the good stuff, don't they? It's great, too, right?"

"Best margarita I've ever had," she admits.

I grin hopefully. "Maybe it's the company that's making you feel that way."

She gives me a playful look. "More likely the ocean view."

"Ouch."

She laughs. "You deserved that one, threatening my innocent margarita like that." She picks up the can and holds it close to her chest playfully for a moment. "So what were Christmases like for you, Dodger? No socks and undies?"

"Christmases?" I ask, since it's the furthest thing from my mind as I sit on this sun-soaked beach. "Oh, they were pretty much the way you'd expect with two brothers. We'd get all torqued up on the candy we'd find in our stockings and by noon, Mom and Dad were playing referee to some argument or scuffle."

"I was an only child. Can't relate to that."

"I *wished* I was an only child for most of my life back then."

"But obviously that changed," she notices.

"Yeah, my brothers and I are pretty close," I admit.

"What changed it?"

"The Army, maybe. Or getting deployed. Nothing like going to a war zone and watching your brothers do the same that makes you think about what life might be like if the worst happens."

"Why did you all join?"

"You'd have to ask my brothers why they joined up. I like to tell people that they were just following in my sainted footsteps, but it's probably not true."

She chuckles lightly. "Well, then, why did *you* join up?"

"Simple. I wanted to be a doctor and the Army foot the bill for medical school."

She shakes her head. "I'm not buying that."

"What?"

"I'm not buying it," she repeats. "You're smart. You could have gotten scholarships like I did. There was something else."

I frown slightly, surprised she would even figure it out. Because I don't even think my brothers thought that deeply about why I joined.

"My birthday is September 9th."

She looks at me again and tilts her head in question.

"So because of 9-11," I begin, "I had some somber birthdays. Because anytime I'd turn on the TV around that date, they'd be replaying the footage of the Twin Towers falling or the devastation at the Pentagon, or the plane that went down in Pennsylvania. I started dreading my birthdays just because I knew that it was a time when thousands of Americans were reliving so much pain."

Her expression softens.

"I guess I just wanted to feel like I was—I don't know— doing something to help protect our country. You could say I wanted to be a Soldier more than I did a doctor," I add. "It just worked out well that I could end up being both."

Eyeing me thoughtfully, she says, "I'll bet you were a good Soldier."

I throw back my head in a laugh. "The worst."

She screws up her face. "Really?"

"Oh, yeah. Fen and Cam were much better at the military thing than me."

"Why?"

"Well, remember how I said I was a bit of a doormat when I was a teen, you know, just sort of letting my dad force me into the idea of being a doctor? Something snapped when I got in the Army and I realized I had some balls. I was contrary all the time. Questioning every order when I thought it was wrong, speaking out when I should have shut up."

She looks stunned. "I can't even picture you that way."

"Picture it, because it's the truth. I might have wanted to be a Soldier when I was a kid, but I was way too much of a know-it-all pain in the ass to be a good one. Fact is, if I wasn't a damn good doctor, I'm sure they would have booted me out."

"But you're not anymore," she notes. "A know-it-all pain in the ass, I mean."

I pull my eyes from the ocean and loll my head to the side to look at her mischievously. "Reach for your phone one more time while you should be relaxing and you'll discover how much of a know-it-all pain in the ass I can be when I toss it into the ocean."

With that, she pulls her phone out of the pocket in her chair and puts it next to her margarita, also out of my reach.

"You're right. Maybe you *are* still a bit that way," she agrees, her eyes transforming to mere slits. "But I'm starting to get used to it."

I soak in the smile she sends me as much as I do her words, unable to resist the hope that she'll get so used to me that she might stick around here. Because whatever the explanation is for my feelings right now, I know I want more of this with her.

More than I can possibly get in the few days she has left here.

CHAPTER 18

~ SAMANTHA ~

I embraced this "relaxation" concept so well yesterday that I'm doing it again today, soaking in the hot tub at Dodger's community pool with Annie. Palm trees sway above lounge chairs and a manmade waterfall flows into the main pool where Cam is playing in the shallow end with Kaila who dons an adorable floatie.

Shaking my head slightly at the opulence around me, I confide, "This sure doesn't look like the community pool where I spent my childhood."

Annie laughs. "I know, right? In my town we had a big rectangular pool in the middle of a hot slab of concrete."

"We must have grown up in the same town then," I say, even though I know we didn't.

"We've got a nice neighborhood pool up where we are, but this one at Dodger's is like a five-star resort. I have to admit, I hope he never sells his place."

My brow furrows. "Do you think he would?"

She pauses thoughtfully, then tosses her shoulders up a bit. "He always says he won't. They've got a lot of sentimental attachment to this place that I honestly don't even understand."

"They bought it together, right?"

"Yep. Dodger bought out Cam and Fen when they moved out though. They didn't even ask him to, but he wanted to make sure that the equity they had here could go toward their own homes." She watches her husband and child in the distance. "But this place is more than just a three-bedroom condo to them, I think. They got it when they were all in the Army, and I think they just needed something concrete to unite them as brothers."

"I don't think it's just a place that holds the three of them together," I consider, thinking about the bond they seem to have. Dodger's home is filled with photographs of their shared experiences together, some in uniform, some from when they were little. But all have that quality that makes something tug at my heart.

"Yeah," Annie agrees. "Their family had a lot to do with it. I mean, the *other* Sheridans. They all get along so well, but I think when Cam was younger, he and his brothers had a bit of that us-versus-them mentality."

"Really?"

"Yeah. Imagine them as teenagers—you know, that age when you can't help but compare yourself to others..." Her voice trails.

I can't help picturing a younger version of myself. "I remember envying people who had two parents in their lives rather than just a mom. Even though Mom was great, I'd still feel that longing sometimes. That jealousy." I sit up a little straighter and look around me. "I can kind of understand why they might have been drawn to this place, then. I mean, this kind of luxury would impress even that other branch of the Sheridan family tree."

"Exactly. But then after that, when they decided to stop renting it out to tourists and use it for themselves, I think it was their—I don't know—their sanctuary after they left the Army. Kind of a place where they could rally together and figure out what they'd do next."

"Ironic," I say with a bit of a scoff.

"What's ironic?"

"I'm using it the same way they did. As a place of refuge." I can't help the frown on my face, despite the fact that my life seems nearly perfect right now, muscles being massaged by jets, glorious weather, and my dear friend here at my side. In just a couple days, I'll be back in DC, facing my unemployed status and a stack of bills that need paying.

"Place of refuge?" She repeats my words, cocking her head. "So I'm guessing Dodger must have taken you to Pu'uhonua o Honaunau yesterday?"

"Where?" From behind my sunglasses, I squint my eyes.

"Pu'uhonua o Honaunau—the Place of Refuge."

"You mean there's an actual place here called that?"

"Yeah—it's amazing," she tells me. "A sacred place. Back in ancient times, if Hawaiians broke the *kapu,* which is the law, the penalty was death. But if they could make it to Pu'uhonua o Honaunau, then they couldn't kill you. It was the place of refuge, literally."

I get chills, despite the hot water that pummels me. Somehow the history here makes me respect the land, the water, the very air I breathe just a little bit more. It's almost as though I'm living in a kind of legend here, playing a role in something beautiful and intimidating at the same time.

"So how are *you* changing from your refuge here, Sam?" she asks, her eyes dead serious.

"What do you mean? I'm still the same as ever."

She gives me a knowing look. "No one walks away from this island unchanged."

Feeling uneasy for some reason, I remind her, "I did the last two times I was here."

Her eyes widen as she counters, "That's because you barely looked up from your phone."

Biting my lip, I cringe. "Yeah. Sorry about that." My eyes stray from hers and look upward at the clear blue sky. "Well, I guess this time away has made me see that I need something in my life other than just work."

"You need *fun*," she says quickly, reading my mind just like she used to back in the days when we'd hang out together in DC.

"Yeah," I agree, but not quite ready to finish the thought out loud. Because while she's right—I do need fun—there's something else I need. Something I don't care to admit to Annie. Or to myself.

I need more of this feeling that Dodger gives me. This stirring from somewhere deep inside me that makes me feel alive in a completely new way.

"So what are you and Dodger doing tonight?" she asks, snapping me out of my thoughts for a moment.

"I'm not sure. He said it's a surprise. But for all the things we've seen on this island, I'm not really sure there can be anything left."

She laughs. "I've lived here for a while now and I'm still finding new things to see. I wish Fen was in town. He'd take you up in his helicopter. It's my favorite way to see the island. You really get a better feel for all the different climates we have here."

"Well, if I saw it all, then I wouldn't have a reason to come back."

Her smile disappears momentarily. "So that's a promise, then? That you'll come back? I mean, I know it will be a while after you start your new job. But you really *will* come back?"

"Promise. I've got you and a goddaughter I have to keep my eye on, you know," I say, finding it a struggle not to mention how much I want to see Dodger again. Because the reality is that he probably will have settled down with someone by then. He's the last of the three brothers to be single. There's bound to be some pressure there.

To distract myself from the thought, my eyes drag over to little Kaila playing with her dad in the distance, and I wonder how big she'll be when I return. "Kaila certainly bounced back from her cold," I notice, forcing a grin.

"Thank goodness. Her new doctor says she's back to 100 percent and Dodger agrees. And he's a bit on the overprotective side."

I laugh, somehow able to guess that about him on my own. "It didn't knock you out long either."

She shakes her head. "I think I barely had it. Just a low fever and none of the drainage issues. But the amount of phlegm that little baby can produce..." She exhales a long, pained breath, looking as though she's drawing an image in her mind right now.

I choke back a laugh. If I had a dollar for every time she mentioned a bodily fluid or excrement of some kind since she became a mom, I'd be a wealthy woman.

Over the hum of the motor and bubbles, Annie sighs. "Babies are like a roller coaster, I'm discovering. When she gets sick, it happens in an instant, and then she recovers just as fast. Same with her moods. She's happy and laughing one minute and then screaming the next." She takes a sip from her water bottle on the ledge behind us. "Reminds me of my mom when she hit menopause."

Now I let the laugh out. "I've missed you, Annie." Again, my eyes fix on Cam who is now playing some kind of peek-a-boo game with Kaila. "I keep trying to hate Cam for taking you away from DC, but he sure makes it hard."

"Well, I can't help pointing out that you could just move here. I mean, I can't imagine there are lobbying jobs on the Big Island, but you could get something."

My muscles, once thoroughly relaxed, tense up just enough for me to take notice. Last night, I got another rejection email from a place that had interviewed me before I left. I'd really hoped for the opposite from them; they had seemed so enthusiastic about my credentials.

Yet this time, I didn't cry about it. This time, I just enjoyed being held by Dodger and assured that it will all work out.

Here in paradise, it's so easy to believe that. It's so easy to relegate my career to a lower priority. When he took me into his arms, it didn't seem to matter to me whether I got the job of my dreams or not. It seemed inconsequential.

I'm not sure if it's the island's influence that's doing that to me. Or if it's all Dodger. But I'm grateful for it.

"I won't deny that the idea has crossed my mind," I finally acknowledge.

She lifts her eyebrows at me.

I shake my head. "But I love what I do. You know that. I can't give it up for an island."

Or for a man, I can't help adding in my mind, thinking of Dodger at work right now and just how much I'm looking forward to him coming home later.

"Or for a man."

When she says it, once again plucking my thoughts from my head, my eyes slash a path straight to hers.

She tilts her head. "Come on, Sam. I *know* you. I can tell you're having *way* too much fun with my brother-in-law."

"Fun," I find myself whispering the word. Yeah, it's been

fun. But there's something more to it than that. When I'm with him, I feel complete inside.

I've never considered myself particularly spiritual. I might be; I truly might. But I never allowed myself the time to even experience it.

Yet when I'm with Dodger I feel like there's something about him that melds so perfectly with me, as though all those things I've heard about an immortal soul really are true, and mine has somehow found its match.

I try to tell myself it's just the island that's doing this to me. That there's something about the way the wind whispers through the palm fronds or the hypnotic sound of the waves as they roll in, caressing the warm sand.

I try to convince myself that it's only a side effect from being in paradise.

But as many times as I tell myself this, there's a voice deep inside of me that warns me that this won't come around twice in a lifetime.

And that I've fallen completely in love with him.

Impractical as it is.

CHAPTER 19

- DODGER -

At 9,200 feet, I'm surprised when my phone rings in my pocket. Up here at the visitors' center for Mauna Kea, there's limited reception to say the least.

"Annie?" I say at the sight of her number. Of the two of them, it's usually Cam who calls me, so I immediately think that there's something wrong. "Everything okay?"

"Hey, Dodger. Everything's fine. I tried calling Sam, but it went straight to voice mail. Is she with you?"

"Yeah. She's in the restroom now. We're at the visitors' center at Mauna Kea."

"Oh, *that's* the surprise Sam mentioned. Good idea. I can't believe I even got you then. I never get a signal up there."

"You and me both. What's up?"

"Cam caught a tuna today so we're grilling it tonight. Do you and Sam want to come over?"

I lift my eyebrows. "Sorry, Sis. The altitude's doing something weird to my brain. I thought I heard you just say Cam actually caught a fish."

"He did."

"You mean someone *he was with* caught one."

"No. *He* did. Dead serious. He says it must be a sign that his luck's changing."

"First off, I don't believe in signs. Second, he's got a gorgeous, brilliant wife, an adorable daughter, and commutes fifteen feet to his home office every day. I don't think my little brother can get any luckier."

"Aw, thanks for the *gorgeous wife* part of that. So you want to join us?"

"Nah," I answer. "We're here for the sunset. It'll be late by the time we make it back down to you."

"Going up to the peak?"

"Yep. I thought I should have Samantha acclimate to the altitude here for a while. But we'll head up in a few."

"Cool. Did you bring your binos?"

"Of course."

She waits a beat before speaking again. "Pretty romantic setting. Maybe you should get down on one knee and convince her to stay here with us."

I laugh only because I know she's not serious. "Absolutely. I mean, I generally wait till I've been with a woman for a full two weeks before making such a proposal. But why the hell not?"

"Actually, I was only half-kidding, Dodger. You guys look pretty good together. And I've never seen either one of you happier. What does it take to convince you? A sign?"

"*Again* with the signs?" I ask her, finally starting to under-stand why my brother is transforming into a sap. "You just want her to stay," I point out, avoiding the fact that I share the sentiment.

"True. But I'd like to see you both get the happily ever after Cam and I did."

"Sis, it takes more than a week or so to get to a happily ever after, you know."

"Not necessarily. When it's right, it's right."

"Samantha's got a life in DC," I say, my tone turning less friendly by the second.

She pauses. "Tell me something, Dodger. Why do you call her Samantha?"

My face contorts at the strange question. "Uh, that's her name."

"Yeah, but Cam and I call her Sam. You call her Samantha."

"I don't know. She looks like a Samantha, I guess."

"No. She looks like a Sam. A *Sam* is practical, just like she always boasts. A *Sam* doesn't want you to even bother wasting breath on a second or a third syllable. Yet you *do* bother."

"Okay… I have no idea where you're going with this."

"Dodger, you call her *Samantha* because you want to make it clear that you don't see her the way Cam and I do. And she doesn't *correct* you because she doesn't see you the way she sees Cam or me. I'd bet that subconsciously, you two have been attracted to each other from the first time you called her Samantha and she said nothing to stop you."

Rolling my head backward on my shoulders, I groan. "Subconsciously, huh? Did you pick that up from one of those parenting books you're always reading?"

She doesn't bother answering. "Seriously, you're cut from the same cloth, the two of you. I never really saw it before because you were both with other people, but seriously, you're birds of a feather."

I can't help the snort. "So I'm a bird and a cloth cutting. You know your theory is lacking when you resort to idioms."

I spot Samantha headed toward me. "Hey, Samantha's back. Do you want to talk to her?"

"Oh, you mean, *Sam's* back?"

"God, will you let up on me?"

"Okay, okay," she laughs. "And no, I don't need to talk to her. Just head up to that peak. You're running out of time if you want to catch sunset, you know. But remember what I said, Dodger. You need to trust destin—"

I cut her off, making fake static noises into the phone. "Sis, you're breaking up. Think we're losing the connection." Then I disconnect, knowing I'll catch hell for it when I return to sea level.

"What was that about?" Samantha asks, her brow furrowed.

"Nothing. Hey, let's hit the road or we'll miss the sunset."

We climb into my Jeep and head up the steep gravel road that leads to the peak. Novices—at least the smart ones—take the safe route and book their trips with a tourist group that does this drive regularly. It takes a pretty competent driver with some four-wheel drive skills to make it, and God knows you're in trouble if you get stranded up here.

I give Samantha one of the parkas that I loaded into my back seat, and she's got some of my sweats covering her legs, cinched tightly at the waist. People generally don't pack things like that when they head to a tropical paradise, but you need it up here above the clouds.

Parked near one of the tourist vans, I get out and help her onto the hood of my Jeep, putting a pillow behind her on the windshield so she can be comfortable. As I pour her some of the hot chocolate from my thermos, she raises her eyebrows at the steam.

"Oh, wow. It's still warm," she observes. "You came prepared. Do this often?"

"I've been up here a dozen or so times, I guess. Give or take a few."

Her eyes turn to the vastness that is stretched out toward the sun, with clouds that lay themselves out like a carpet beneath us, and she breathes out a sigh. "For most people, this would be considered a once-in-a-lifetime event, saying good-bye to the sun from up here."

"Not if you lived here," I can't help myself from saying. "If you lived here, you'd do it anytime you wanted." *If you lived here...* my words continue to echo in my head. I might pretend I'm speaking rhetorically, but it's not the truth. I'm like Annie that way. I want her to stay, too. Just for different reasons.

Very different reasons.

Glancing at her, I look for any trace of interest in the idea. I can't help it. Yet her expression is completely serene and unreadable.

Eventually, she says quietly, "Maybe one day, I'll be watching the sunset from the Capitol building steps at the same time you're watching it from up here."

"A nice sentiment. But with the time difference, it's not really possible," I can't help pointing out, logical guy that I am.

"Of course. I kind of forgot about that. Maybe that altitude is doing something to my brain, after all." She laughs.

I drape my arm over her. "How about this? When you're sitting on those Capitol steps at the end of the day looking at the sunset, I'll sit with my afternoon coffee fix, and I'll watch it with you."

"It seems odd, really, doesn't it? So much distance between us?"

"It does," I agree. Especially right now, I consider, I could be convinced that we were never meant to be apart.

I want to say that to her. I'd love to. I'd love to end this day by just giving in to the sentimentality that both my sisters-in-law are always pushing on my brothers. It would be easy to do when I'm with Samantha.

I've spent my life believing that love is nothing more than the right mix of chemicals secreted in the brain. As a doctor, I know the reality of that. I can rattle off every one of them—vasopressin and oxytocin among my personal favorites—and the areas of the brain that they effect.

But this feeling in my gut just doesn't mesh with what I learned in medical school. It's more of an instinct, as though some innate part of me recognizes that if I was truly meant for someone, then that someone would be Samantha.

Even though it's completely illogical to feel this way after such a short time together, I do. I have no control over that fact.

But I'd look foolish to her—to me, too—especially when I remind myself that she's leaving. Still, I want to say something.

"Why do people call you Sam?" I find myself asking instead.

She shrugs. "I don't know. It just suits me better, I guess."

But it doesn't, I want to say. Because I seem to lack the ability to call her that, and I refuse to believe the reason is the one Annie gave to me. "Do you mind that I call you Samantha?"

"No, I don't mind." She looks thoughtful for a moment. "It sort of suits *you*, I guess."

I warm inside at her simple statement. Because even if Annie's theory is ridiculous, I can't help liking the fact that I get to call Samantha something different from everyone else.

As the sun nears the horizon, she pulls out her iPhone to record this last minute of daylight. It's looks surreal up here above the clouds; The amber sunlight stretches out its arms along the horizon as though it's reluctant to disappear—like it wants an end to this day as little as I do.

But time wins out.

Touching her finger to her phone, she turns off her camera after the last rays give way to darkness. "Now I can have a perfect Hawaiian sunset whenever I want," she says.

Leaning over, I kiss her because I always want her to remember that *I* was the one up here with her on this mountain peak watching the day end in the most glorious fashion. I kiss her until the darkness consumes the wide, open sky. When our lips finally part, stars above us remind us that even the nights here hold beauty and promise.

I pull out my binoculars and we take in the cosmos, all so much more visible in the clear, thin air. And, as often happens on the island of aloha, a couple of the tourist groups adopt us into their fold, letting us share the telescopes they've set up. Samantha lights up when she sees her first binary star and is giddy at the sight of the rings of Saturn.

As always, I'm struck by the fact that all the amazing things a person can see on this planet pale in comparison to what the universe holds for us.

Yet it feels different this time. With Samantha at my side, I've discovered I'm capable of feeling something that stretches further than the most distant object we can spot through any telescope.

For a person like me, that sets my reality on edge.

I'm completely in love with her.

I want every day to end like this. With her at my side. I can take anything life has in store for me, so long as I can have her.

While every neuron in my brain is insisting that this must be the effects of the low oxygen level up here, there's something else in me that's telling me the exact opposite.

"Best. Day. Ever," she whispers to me, punctuating each of the three words with a soft kiss to my lips.

I find myself wishing it was three *other* little words she felt inspired to say to me right now. Because maybe then she'd consider staying here on the island forever with me. But taking what I can get, I lean in to kiss her one more time.

Just as our lips part, a meteor streaks across the sky. She sucks in a breath. "Oh my God! Did you see that?" she cries out right along with several tourists nearby. "I've never seen a meteor before."

I have. Lots of times, though I don't tell her that. Contrary to what people think, they're actually predictable here where the skies are clear, if you keep your eye on any meteor calendar you can find online.

But to me, that wasn't a meteor.

It was a sign.

A sign that I've lost my sense of reason. And just now, I'm okay with that.

We drive home in the pitch darkness, taking the road slowly, right along with the tourist vans in front and behind us. Safety in numbers up here on the mountain, and without any trace of cell reception at the peak, it's the smart way to keep things.

I'm not anxious to end this night. Not even now, so late after a full day of work at the clinic. But it's not just because it's been a great day. It's because she'll be going home soon, and I'm not quite ready yet for her to leave.

What if she didn't?

I glance over at her for barely an instant; it's not smart to pull your eyes from the road here. But I can't resist.

What if she extended her stay? I can buy her a new ticket home. And can't she send out her resume from here just as easily as she does from there?

I stew on the thought for a few minutes, just until we pass

the sign for the visitors' center and it serves as a reminder to me that the reality of life at sea level awaits us. And in our reality, there's only one day left of her trip.

I need more time with her. Time to sift through all these feelings.

Time to figure out if there is anything about my island home that might persuade her to give up a career that means so much to her.

When I open my mouth to ask her if she'd stay longer, I'm stopped by the sound of her cell.

"Hey—I've got a signal again!" she chirps happily.

I give my head a shake. "Still the cell phone addict you always were."

She grins at me, reaching into her purse. "Don't knock it. You were once the same way." She glances down, frowns at the number she sees on her display, and holds it up to her ear to listen for the voicemail.

I'm quiet while she listens, then after just a few seconds, she gasps, "Oh my God!"

"Everything okay?" Again, the doctor in me assumes it's bad news. I really do need to stop doing that.

Still listening, she holds up a finger to me, silencing me. Then I see her grin appear, slowly widening.

When I do, I somehow know what's being said to her in that voicemail.

She got a job offer.

And I've lost my chance.

CHAPTER 20

~ SAMANTHA ~

I stretch out my legs on Annie's chaise lounge in their backyard, the salt from another margarita still stinging my lips as I watch the wild goats eat the tall grasses that border her backyard.

This is the life.

Right now, I can almost forget that I'm leaving tomorrow. Right now, I can pretend that this is my life right here and that Dodger will still be mine tomorrow and the tomorrow after that. And all the ones that follow.

Yes, I can imagine it so clearly—a temptation that is out of my reach—one that is further complicated by the fact that I should be overjoyed right now.

I accepted a job—a great one. And if I was the same person who arrived here nearly ten days ago, I'd feel nothing but excitement as I look forward to embarking on a new challenge.

But I'm not the same person.

"Shoo!" Annie orders the goats, but her command lacks gusto.

Glancing at my friend, I see her frowning at the animals.

"But they're so cute," I tell her. "Why don't you like them?"

"Because they eat everything in my yard."

"But they're so *cute*," I repeat, noticing the slight whine in my voice.

"Yep. *Cute* pests." She juts her chin in the direction of the neighbor's yard. "They were smart and just put in fencing. But I hate to do that because it destroys the view."

My eyes track from the goats to the blue water in the distance. From up at this elevation, I can see just enough of the ocean to remind me that yes, I'm still in paradise. "Yeah, I wouldn't block the view either. If I could get a view like that, I think I'd stay here forever."

Her eyes snap to mine and I swear I see her ears perk up.

"Hold on a sec. Were you being serious? I mean, I can't help hoping…" Her voice trails.

"Hoping I'd stay?" My shoulders heave a sigh. "You know I can't. Especially not now that I have a job waiting for me at home. Besides, there's no place for a federal lobbyist here. And this job I just accepted—it's everything I'd hoped for." And it *is*, I remind myself. So much so that I stayed awake until three a.m. Hawai'i time this morning so that I could call them to accept the position the moment they opened their office on the East Coast of the mainland.

I glance at her, and she looks unconvinced.

"I mean, lobbying for kids with cancer… that's going to feel incredible." I tell myself that I'm reminding her, but maybe I'm reminding myself. "I'll feel like I'm making a difference again, you know? I've missed that."

"Yeah, I kind of knew you'd say that." She offers me a half-hearted smile. "How much vacation time do you get?"

I perk up at the thought. "Three weeks. They offered me two at first, but I talked them up to three when they couldn't go any higher on my salary."

She grins. "Now that's the Sam I know and love. And you'll come back to visit us, right? I've kind of gotten used to having you around. And so has Dodger," she adds, giving me a weighted look.

Suddenly uncomfortable, I find myself standing and walking toward the border of her yard. The goats flee about twenty feet, then resume their grazing as I look out to the blue horizon in the distance. "Annie, he'll find someone else before I get back here. And I really want you to know, I'm okay with that," I lie.

Like a rug.

"Are you so sure about that?"

I force myself to turn to her. "Of course I'm sure. I don't want things being awkward between us. So when it happens, don't feel you need to hide anything from me." My voice actually catches as I say it, suddenly picturing myself showing up at a barbeque like tonight and seeing Dodger arm-in-arm with someone else. Then one day, I'll visit again and see a beautiful baby in his arms, like a testament to the love that could have been mine if I had just given it some more time to blossom.

And me? I'll have my stack of business cards with an impressive job title to comfort me.

Stubbornly, my eyes lock onto hers like I'm in a staring contest, trying to show her that I really mean what I say. But then I feel the sting behind my eyes and glance away, turning my back to her.

I lose the staring contest. And I lose Dodger.

This just isn't the best way to spend my final night on the Big Island.

"Oh, wow. You're really in love with him." I hear Annie's

voice behind me.

Was there ever any doubt? I want to bark it at her. "I'm not," I deny instead, unable to face her when I say it.

"You are. I mean, I kind of knew already, but I didn't realize how much."

I blink back the moisture until my eyes are clear and bright again. And determined. Very determined.

"I can't be in love with him. People don't fall in love that fast, Annie. Lust, maybe. But not love."

"This has got to be hard for you, hon."

My shoulders droop at the softness of her voice. *Please, oh please, God, don't let Cam come back out here after he finishes changing Kaila's diaper. Because the tears are coming now, and I can't seem to stop them.*

My friend comes up behind me and drapes an arm over my shoulder.

"It shouldn't be hard for me," I tell her. "That's the thing that's driving me crazy. Because my whole life is forty-five hundred miles away from here. It's not like I'm going to give up a career and a place I love for a man I've known for what... ten days?"

"Because that's something your mother would have done."

I stiffen. "My mother never would have done that. She never allowed herself to fall in love in the first place because she had a kid to take care of."

Even with my eyes still fixed on the ocean, I sense she's shaking her head.

"I don't mean *after* she had you," she says. "I mean *before*. Isn't that what happened between her and your dad?"

Stepping away from her, my body deflates into a nearby chair. "'Just don't do what I did,' Mom would tell me, Annie. Still does, actually. 'Just use your brain and not your heart.' That's all I ever heard growing up."

"Good things can happen when you use your heart. Hey

—" She sits next to me and gives my hand a squeeze. "—despite the failure your parents' relationship must have been, *you* came out of it. And I'm sure glad to have you."

Another tear trickles down my cheek and I'm just tired enough not to wipe it away. "I used to wonder about that, actually. Sometimes when I'd see all the regret in her eyes as she'd talk about my dad. And yeah, he was a deadbeat. There's no getting around that. But when I was little especially, I'd wonder sometimes if she regretted having me the same way she regretted marrying my father."

"You know that's not true. You get along so well with your mom." She pauses and a slight grin betrays her. "Well, when she's not lecturing you about the importance of your career or forwarding you stuff that she thinks will make you invaluable at work."

A laugh escapes me. "You know my mother so well."

"Yeah, and I was there when she gave you your first briefcase for your birthday. Remember? And she didn't do that because she wanted you to be some wild DC success while carrying it. She got it because she loves you and is proud of you. Believe me, she might regret that she needed to marry your dad to bring you into her life. But that woman would have married a snake to have you."

"She kind of did," I scoff, suddenly remembering that day when she gave me that gift. I still use that beautiful leather briefcase today—and it's not lost to me just how many hours she had to put in to pay for it. "And I know she was only trying to really ingrain in me how important a career is. And I'm grateful for it because now I have a job I think I'll really love waiting for me back home."

"It sounds like it's going to be everything you hoped for."

"Yeah," I say thoughtfully. "But this whole experience here has made me see how much I need other things in my life other than just work. Because a job can be taken away so easily."

"So, what is it you want?"

I give a quick glance around me at Annie's cheerful yard and house. At the barbeque, the box of beach toys, and the weedy little garden Annie's struggling to grow. I see the playpen that they dragged out here before we ate, and even the goats that are still mocking my friend as they eat away at her grass.

Then I see Cam through the glass of the sliding door, reaching for its handle with their baby in his arms, until his eyes meet Annie's. And in that one brief glance at his wife, he instinctively knows she wants him to leave us alone just now. So he disappears into the house again.

And *I want that*.

I want a man who knows me so well he can understand what I want before I can even say it.

I want a man who loves me so much that I don't have to fear the love that I give back to him, because I know he will always be there.

And right now, I want enough time with Dodger to find out if he might share this feeling I have, this feeling that all of our tomorrows could somehow be even brighter if we shared them together.

But I can't have that.

"I want to see the Smithsonian museums," I say instead, feeling resolute that I won't let the disappointment of leaving Dodger be the only thing I take away from paradise.

Her eyes widen, surprised by my answer. "The Smithsonian museums?"

"Yeah. I want to take every Saturday and see a different one until I run out."

She sends me an odd look. "Well, that sounds doable."

"And I want to go on one of those farm tours they have in Loudon County. Remember those? The ones we'd always read about in the *Post* but never had time to do?"

She smiles, and I hope she's as warmed as I am by the memory of her sitting at my tiny kitchen counter in my old apartment talking about all the things we'd do that weekend if we could just find the time or the money. "Yes, I remember those," she whispers.

But there's no longing in her tone the way there is in mine, and I know that all her dreams are here now, in Hawai'i, just where they should be.

My lips curve downward, still thinking. "And I think I want to take up rowing."

"Rowing?"

"Yeah. You know... at one of those rowing clubs we've got in DC. I think I need more water in my life," I add, gazing out to the ocean again. "I mean, the Potomac River's not exactly..." My voice trails looking for the right word.

"Blue?" Annie suggests.

I narrow my eyes, finally feeling a little more like myself. "Hey, no need to get all snobby on me just because you've got —well... that." I gesture out to the ocean. "I was just going to say the Potomac's not exactly the Pacific. But it's better than nothing."

She laughs. "Hawai'i has changed you."

"No," I find myself confessing. "That was all Dodger."

When I drive back to Dodger's from Annie's house, I'm struck by how familiar it all seems, this path I take from her place to his, as though I should be doing this regularly. As if that condo on the beach has become more than just a place I'm staying for a while. It feels like home to me.

What terrifies me most is that it's not the building or the location or the soft bed that awaits me. It's not even the lanai or the view of the ocean or how the sound of the waves makes me feel like anything is possible in this life.

It's Dodger that's making me feel this way. It's the fact that when I slip between the sheets tonight, I know he'll join me in just a few hours after he gets home from work. I know I'll feel his arm drape over me as he holds me close, and I know with that one gesture alone, he'll make me feel like I'm loved even if it's too early for him to say such a thing to me.

And after I settle into bed and hear the door open and shut downstairs, he does just that.

His skin seems to meld to mine as he slips beneath the light duvet. When he silently slides up close to me, I whisper, "How was work?"

It feels so natural. So right. As though it's the way I should always greet him.

"You're awake," he answers.

"No. I'm talking in my sleep," I joke. I roll over and etch the image of him in the dim light into my soul.

His sly grin emerges. "Really? What else can you do in your sleep?"

I nibble my lip. "How about we find out together?"

He dips his face to mine, tasting me, consuming me. He's naked already, and seems to have developed the habit of sleeping in the nude these past days, for which I'm eternally grateful.

I'm just as grateful for his hands, and how adeptly they take my panties off me without him even needing to stop kissing me. Somehow, he manages to slip on a condom while barely missing a beat. And he slides inside me as though he's a perfect fit.

Because he is.

We move in unison, wordlessly this time, and so slowly it makes me think we're both memorizing the sensation of our joining. Tonight, it feels so different, knowing that tomorrow I'll be leaving.

I push away the worries of it. I deny myself the right to picture things between us when I return and how it will undoubtedly be different.

I absolve myself of the practicality that I used to take pride in.

Right now, I'm just making love to a man who, in a different plane of reality, would be destined for me.

I take him in deeper with each thrust, my heartbeat not frantic like it usually is when I have sex with him. Now, there's not that flash of heat between us. It's more of a warmth this time, as his kisses trace a line from my lips to my breasts and then ever so slowly, back to my mouth again.

He pulls me over to my side and nudges my leg up higher on his hip. His lips part from mine and we just watch each other quietly as he moves in and out of me. My gaze on him absorbs every intricacy of his face and body, the way his eyes flash softly when the tip of him strikes my innermost depth, the way his fingers feel as he strokes my breast, the way the two tiny veins in his forehead seem to become more pronounced the closer he comes to his release.

We stay like this for what seems like hours, just enjoying the fact that we're together in the most intimate way, not ready to complete the act and not anxious to part our bodies.

And certainly not eager to part altogether when I step onto a plane that will take me home.

When I can no longer deny the climax that builds inside me like a beautiful storm, I don't cry out with release like I usually do. Instead, I keep my lips pressed tight because I know the only words I could possibly say to him right now are not allowed.

I love you.

I love you, Dodger, and I'll never stop.

I keep those words inside me even as he gives in to his own desire along with me, and then holds me close the rest of the night.

I'll keep those words inside me forever, etched in my heart, long after he's found someone new. They'll comfort me.

I have to believe, they'll comfort me.

CHAPTER 21

- DODGER -

Flights to the mainland around this time of year tend to be red-eyes, leaving after sunset. Some tourists say they love this because it gives them more time to enjoy the island. But I've heard others say that it's the worst possible way to end a vacation here.

I never understood why until now.

Because there's a kind of dread that comes with ending a perfect time in Hawai'i. For tourists, I imagine the thought of leaving paradise can make every ray of sunshine on their last day, every gentle wave along the shore, and every peal of laughter on the sandy beach seem like painful reminders that their time is coming to an end.

It's the same way I feel right now, driving Samantha to the airport.

I'd volunteered to take her here myself because Baby K

will be sound asleep right now. And truth be known, I need to do this on my own—just to show myself that I can.

I *can* let her go.

"Did you pack those chocolates in your carry-on?" I ask, thinking those chocolate-covered macadamia nuts she bought yesterday might very well get brutalized in her checked baggage.

"Yeah."

"That was a good idea, by the way. Bringing them into your new office," I add, keeping my voice as even as I can. "That will make a good first impression, you know?"

She pauses a moment. "It was kind of my mom's idea, actually."

"Smart woman," I tell her, almost adding how much I'd like to meet her one day. But that would be too personal. There will be no reason for me to meet the woman who raised Samantha into the capable, compassionate person she is. And that annoys the hell out of me.

"It was so hard saying good-bye to Annie this afternoon," she barely whispers it, as if she's saying it more to herself than to me. "Kaila will probably be so much bigger when I come back."

I don't point out that it's a statement she's said two other times this evening. We had dinner on the beach with Cam and the family, and Samantha couldn't take her eyes off the way Baby K takes to the water, giggling every time a gentle wave rolled in and touched her toes.

"Any idea when that might be?" I dare to ask.

"Well, I need to settle in and accrue the vacation time. Maybe nine months or so."

Nine months. In nine months, so much can change. Even if a guy doesn't want it to. In nine months, she'll probably find some slick DC businessman who wears an Armani suit rather than a tropical shirt like the one I've got on. Some guy who will take her to some of those five-star restaurants they've got there which might make an evening on the lanai under the stars pale in comparison.

I hate that guy, whoever he is.

If I didn't feel so damn deeply toward her, I might have been able to pull out some jovial tone right now and say something like, *"Well, if you don't have a boyfriend or husband by then, I'd be happy to pick this up where we left off when you return."*

But I find myself unwilling to minimize what we've shared by saying such a thing right now, even if it might make all this less awkward when I next see her. Because, dammit, this wasn't just some hook-up based on convenience.

Not to me.

And I really don't think to her.

I turn into the parking lot and look for a space. Inwardly, I'm cursing security protocols that make her arrive two hours early for her flight and won't allow me to sit with her at the gate until she boards.

Even more, I hate that I'm going to have to drive away and not tell her that I love her. That I want her to stay. That I want her to give up her job and make her life right here where she's been happy these past ten days.

But love can't be selfish.

"So you're sure you'll be ready to start work the day after tomorrow?" I ask instead of pouring my soul out to her. "I mean, you remember what jetlag can do to a person."

"I'll be okay. It'll probably be better for me to just hit the ground running. And they need me right away. They were using a firm, but couldn't justify the expense of it to their constituents. So it's important that they get someone like me back on the Hill for them before they lose any steam."

I can't help smiling. She sounds like she's from DC again.

No longer talking about the waves and the moon and the dolphins. She's becoming the person she needs to be to thrive in that city again, and I should be happy to see it.

If I really love her, then I should be happy.

So I tell myself I am.

"So you're headed to Oʻahu this week?" she asks in a light tone that suggests she's just trying to fill the air.

Somehow I hate the idea that it's come to that. That this woman who once shared some of her innermost thoughts feels the need to reduce our relationship to small talk. Is this what it will be like when she returns to visit Cam and Annie?

I force myself to answer. "Yeah. I told Fen I'd help him paint a few rooms in their new house." I nearly snort at my words. "Can't really call it a *new* house, though, come to think of it. Not with those appliances they need to replace."

"Let me guess. Harvest gold color."

I smile at her. "How'd you guess?"

"My grandma had the same ones."

I sigh. "It's a fixer upper, that's for sure. But you just can't get a lot for your money on Oʻahu. You double your mortgage and cut your square footage in half."

"That's what I always heard about it there." She presses her lips together after I pull into a parking space.

So this is it. I'd swear we're both thinking it as we sit here in my Jeep, staring at an airport that we just don't want to be at right now.

"You're going to take that city by storm," I say, forcing a grin as I get out of the car. She opens her own door, beating me to it. But I'm in time to extend a hand to her as she gets out of my Jeep.

And dammit if I don't feel that sensation again. Just the touch of her hand makes the hairs on the back of my neck stand upright.

I remember feeling it that moment when I first touched her at this airport ten days ago.

I remember it when we first enjoyed the stars together, that night when she was so reluctant to let Hawai'i into her soul.

And I remember it from every time we'd make love, grasping her hands against the cool sheets and moving with her in unison.

Damn, this is going to hurt.

"You really don't have to walk me in, you know," she says as I tug one of the bags from her grasp.

"Don't be ridiculous. I can at least get you up to security. I wish I could stay with you till you leave."

"It's okay. There's a lot of reading I need to do anyway. And I've got my laptop."

I chuckle. "Back in a serious relationship with your laptop again? I should feel jealous." I *do* feel jealous, I want to say, of anything and everything that has her attention other than me.

"Hey, I think *my laptop* was getting jealous of *you*," she points out.

I stay with her until she checks in, releasing her luggage to the airline's care. And just this once, I'm wishing that the line was longer so we could spend just a few more minutes together.

She spent the bulk of the day with Cam, Annie, and Baby K finally checking out that coffee farm tour she showed interest in.

I had hated that I was on the schedule at work this morning. What's the sense in owning a clinic if I can't call off work when I damn well please?

I was the one who was with her when she learned about that tour. *I* should get to show her it. I feel childish as I think it, as though I'm five years old again and stomping my feet.

But the fact is, she makes me feel that way—like I want to be indulgent and do as I please, because what I please would be spending my entire day and night with her. And *what I please* would be flinging her over my shoulder right now, plopping her back into my Jeep and taking her home where she belongs, caveman-style.

Which isn't generally the way I roll.

I walk her to just beyond the end of the security line and glance at my watch, wishing I could prolong this somehow. "You sure you've got everything?" I ask.

Please say you forgot something—so that I can drive you right back to where you belong and we can find it together. Even if it takes a lifetime.

"I think so," she replies, barely a whisper.

"Well, if you did forget anything, let me know and I'll send it to you, okay?"

"I will."

"And um, if you don't mind, pop us a text when you touch down, okay?" I request cautiously, as though it might be too much to ask her to do it just for my benefit alone.

"Us?"

"Yeah, me, Annie, Cam." The people who care about you, I want to add. The people who want you to stay.

"Oh, yeah, I will." She puffs out her cheeks and expels a sigh. "Dodger, this—this was really something special."

Was. I hate the word on her lips right now. So I say at least a hint of what's in my heart. "It *is*," I respond. Because I can't stand here and act like my feelings for her are all in the past tense.

She nibbles her lower lip. "I know we acted like this was just a fling, but it's not that to me."

I shake my head slowly, daring to stroke a finger along the curve of her chin. "It never was a fling to me."

She shakes her head. "It was the best ten days of my life,

actually." Her voice cracks and I see her eyes sparkle with unshed tears.

It kills me to see it. Because right now, she should be excited to go home. She has the job that she was hoping for. She has a life she enjoys in a place that inspires her and makes her feel valued. It was something I almost envied about her when I first saw that fire in her eyes as she'd talk about her career. I know the power of that; I can't take it away from her so that she can come here and feel as uninspired in her work as I do at my clinic.

I hate knowing that she should be happy right now, and that what we shared together is ruining that.

I cup her face in my hands, stroking away the tears with my thumbs.

"You are going to do amazing things in that new job, you know. It's just what you wanted. I'd even say you were destined for it, if I believed in that sort of thing," I add with a chuckle and am rewarded by the slightest hint of her smile as though we're sharing an inside joke. Because she's practical the same way I'm logical.

Cut from the same cloth. Just like Annie said.

"You think so?"

"I know so," I confirm. "And you know it, too. Ten days ago, you would have been racing to that plane with this new job waiting for you. This island is inside of you now. It's changed you just like it did me. But you can take that back with you to where you can make your mark on the world."

I kiss her, the touch of her lips against mine devastating me because I know it will be the last time. Her mouth yields to me and I pull her close at her waist. Then I taste her, memorizing the sensation of it. Letting it etch itself into my soul.

After our lips part, I touch my forehead to hers. "Hawai'i will still be here for you when you need it," I remind her, adding in my most logical tone, "barring any unforeseen disasters."

She laughs. "Always with the disclaimers. I'll miss that about you."

I'll miss everything about you. I exhale slowly, trying to muster the selfishness I need to tell her how I feel. *I'll miss you and I don't want you to go.*

But the tears in her eyes remind me I can't. She's already torn, and I don't want that for her. She's going to a job—to a place—that won't allow distractions outside of work. I want her to succeed in it.

I wipe away another rogue tear as it makes a path down her cheek. "You know, since you're leaving, it would be considerate if you could at least not look so damn beautiful when you cry."

She sniffles and blinks several times. "I'd argue with you about that. I've seen what I look like when I cry."

I shake my head. "You look perfect. You *are* perfect. And don't you ever let anyone tell you otherwise."

"Thank you," she whispers.

"For what?"

"For the compliment. For the condo. The beach. The snorkeling. The stargazing. The sightseeing." Her smile builds as she lists it all, then pauses, looking a little devilish. "And that's not even mentioning all the rest."

"I loved every minute of it," I say, letting that critical word slip from my lips and hoping that, on some level, she knows that it's not only the *time* with her that I loved.

It's her. It's all her.

I touch my lips to her forehead and breathe her in one last time, knowing that if she doesn't walk away right now, I might beg her to stay. "Now you go knock 'em dead."

Our eyes meet for a long, weighted moment, as all the

questions, all the emotions that are inside of me are right there in her eyes, reflecting back at me.

She presses her lips together and gives my arm a light squeeze.

Then, with a quick nod of her head, she takes her carry-on bag and walks into the security line.

And unknowingly, takes my heart with her.

I retreat to my parking space, sitting in the car for at least fifteen minutes, just in case... just in case she might send me a text that she's changed her mind.

Of course she doesn't.

So I pull out and head to the Queen K Highway heading home.

CHAPTER 22

~ SAMANTHA ~

"Next time you're crying alone, no matter where you are, I want you to find me. Whether I'm in the next room, or on the other end of a phone call."

I remember Dodger telling me that. He made me promise it, threatening to dump my margarita if I didn't.

I thought about those words so many times on the two flights that took me back to my familiar DC.

But it's hard to make a phone call to a man when you're crying in the lavatory of a plane thirty-five thousand feet above the ground.

In fact, by the time I touched down at Baltimore-Washington International Airport, I was so used to crying on my own that it probably rendered the promise I had made null-and-void.

Even now, as I stand in the bathroom stall at my new office and let a single, renegade tear fall at the passing thought of him, I don't feel guilty that I'm not keeping my promise and calling him.

We've both moved on in that way people must when they're a half a planet away from each other.

Other than the text I sent him when I arrived home, I've miraculously mustered the ability to not send him any more texts... to not call just to hear his voice... to not start a Skype conversation just because seeing him might make my world seem a little more complete.

I am the epitome of practicality once again.

Or at least I'm trying to be.

It certainly helped that I started work so quickly. When I accepted the job, I knew I'd need the immediate distraction of it—something to fill my brain so that I'm not thinking about the sunshine and sand.

And Dodger.

I'd been right about that. Now that I've just gotten done with my first day on the job, I'm so grateful to have spent the last nine hours with constant interruptions and meetings and that unique chaos that comes with a lobbying career.

Because standing here in the bathroom is really the only moment I've had to think about how much I'd rather be in Dodger's arms.

Dabbing my eyes with a little toilet paper, I emerge from the stall.

I look at myself in the mirror in my pantsuit, armed with my briefcase that holds a new stack of business cards. I don't even resemble the woman I was on the island. And while I don't look like Hawai'i ever happened to me, I do know that enough has changed inside of me that when I sit on those Capitol steps tonight to watch the sunset, I'm giving myself more than my usual ten minutes to do it.

"Hey, you headed out?" A co-worker says when she comes into the restroom.

"Yep," I tell her, thinking how the old me would have said, *"No, I'm just going to step out for a bit and come back for a couple more hours at work."*

No longer will I define my day by work alone.

She gives a nod. "Well, congrats on a good day. We're really happy to have you here."

"Thanks. I'm glad to be here. See you tomorrow," I say and head out.

Outside the building, the hues of the evening sky reflect on the cityscape. I used to love evenings in DC, the way the city comes to life in a different way from the rest of the day. At this time, you can still see people in suits like myself, heading to their homes after a long day of work. But you also see people in formalwear coming out of the Metro—because *yes*, it's the norm to take public transportation here while wearing a gown that cost a grand or two—heading to one of the many galas and events that occur every night of the week, whether it's a Friday, Saturday, or even a mundane Wednesday.

I glance at the time on my phone and call my mother. Now that I can officially say I'm working again, I feel safer telling her about my job change.

As that thought occurs to me, I realize how genuinely messed up that really is.

I used to tell my mother everything. Why didn't I tell her I lost my job, especially when it meant so much to me?

"Hi, honey!" she answers. I swear she sounds a lot more relaxed when I'm not on the other side of the world.

"Hey, Mom. I just, uh, wanted to tell you that I started a new job today."

There's a distinct pause on the other end. "A new job?" she asks, clearly baffled. "I thought you loved your old job."

"I—" I stop momentarily—not just my words, but my feet

too, planting them firmly on the concrete for a moment on 6th Street.

I had planned to simply tell her that it was time for a new challenge. It would worry her too much, hearing that I'd lost my job, I had told myself. I don't want her thinking that I'm vulnerable that way.

But then I remember how strong she was, raising me alone. How much courage she had. Can I really say that I'm lying to her to protect her, when it's more likely I'm just trying to protect my stupid pride?

"I, uh, did love my job, Mom. But last month, we lost a couple clients."

"Oh, no," she whispers as if she already knows where this is headed.

"Yeah, I, uh, got laid off. Me and a few others."

"Oh, honey, why didn't you tell me?"

Because I didn't want to worry you. I hear my pat answer formulate in my head. But I don't let the words pass from my lips. "Because I felt—I don't know. Ashamed, maybe."

"Ashamed? Honey, losing a job just happens sometimes. You know how many times I've lost jobs in my life. And it sure wasn't because I wasn't working hard."

"I know. But you always told me I need to focus on my career, you know? You really drummed that into me. And you were right," I quickly add, not wanting her to think she did something wrong in this. Because it was a good lesson she taught me. "I just felt like you'd be—disappointed in me, I guess."

I hear an audible gasp from her. Literally—a full-blown gasp.

"Sweetheart, I could never be disappointed in you. Do you understand that? Never. You are my brilliant, caring, accomplished daughter and I was proud of you when you worked for that firm, and I would have said I was just as proud of you the day you got laid off."

"Thanks, Mom."

She sighs. "I probably focus too much on your career when we talk, honey. It's just—you're grown now, and it's not like I get to cut out construction paper or newspaper clippings for some project you're working on for school or iron on your patches for your scout uniform. I guess I just talk about your job and send you all those stupid articles I read because I'm trying to stay a part of your life."

I resume my walk. "Well, truth is, there really hasn't been that much to talk about in my life other than work. It's all I ever did." I can't help noticing how easily I used the past tense when I said those last words, and I smile because of it. "I'm actually going to try to spend some time doing things other than just working." I say it almost cautiously, wondering how she'll react.

"I think that's wonderful. Much healthier, too. Is that why you went to Hawai'i, then? Not just to see Annie and the baby?"

"I didn't think so at the time. But maybe." I turn onto Pennsylvania Avenue and the Capitol building comes into view. Looking at it now, I remember that first time I told Dodger about coming here at sunset. I remember the feel of being in his arms that morning, stretched out on the bed as we listened to the surf breaking outside the window.

I realize just then how much else I want to tell my mother about my trip. But instead, a question comes out. "Do you really think falling in love is a bad thing?"

There's dead silence for a moment. "Mom?" I ask.

"Um, I'm sorry. That question kind of came out of the blue. Why do you ask?"

"Just answer, Mom. Please. I'd really like to know."

I hear a long sigh.

"Honey, I don't honestly know. It just was bad for me. Bad because it was the wrong man at the wrong time. You're different from me, though. And you're in a different place in your life. So I'd like to think that for you, falling in love could be something special." There's a pause. "So I take it you met someone?"

I frown. "It was Dodger, actually. Cam's brother. And I fell pretty hard."

"And was it a bad thing?" she asks, repeating the question I'd just asked her.

"From where I stand right now, it sucks. Because he's there, and I'm here. He's got a clinic on the island, and I've got a career that needs me to be in DC. When I was there, it all seemed incredible and surreal and now, I just feel empty inside."

"That definitely sounds like love, then. But I will tell you something good about love that I learned from my experience with your father."

My eyes widen at the words. In my thirty years, I've never pictured my mother having anything good to say about something that came from that time with him.

"Even when it doesn't bring you what you wanted—even when you walk away with a broken heart," she begins, "some amazing things can come from it."

I screw up my face. "What things?"

She laughs. "You, honey. I'm talking about you. If I didn't fall in love, I wouldn't have you."

My heart, which had felt pretty damn empty up until two seconds ago, fills to capacity and it stays that way for the rest of my conversation with my mom as I walk along Pennsylvania Avenue.

I make plans to drive up north to her next month and close our conversation when I reach the steps of the Capitol building.

Sliding my phone back into my briefcase, I trot up the stairs.

It feels different this time, knowing I'll linger here as long as I like—enjoying that I don't feel the tug of work urging me to head right back to the office where I'll tap away at my computer until ten p.m.

Sitting on a step, I watch the sun track lower in the sky, making all the buildings along the Mall seem to glow with the warmth of twilight. My eyes take in the structures and I quietly pick out which museum I'll visit this weekend, in lieu of heading into the office to impress my boss.

No. My weekends are my own now. It's better I establish that right from the start.

I glance to either side of me. I'm not alone here. As usual, there are others who share these steps with me, watching the day end. It's the same as on Hawai'i in that small way, how people stop what they are doing to see the sun finish its track across our sky.

My mind journeys back to one very perfect sunset at the peak of Mauna Kea, looking out over a carpet of clouds.

It's around lunchtime in Hawai'i. Dodger is on O'ahu now, I recall, visiting his brother and new sister-in-law.

He might be sitting on their lanai or on the beach. He might be looking at the sun right now.

I remember what we said that evening on Mauna Kea. I might have been a little loopy from the thin air, but I remember every word. And I wonder if he's looking at the sun right now, picturing me here, sitting on the Capitol steps like I said I always do.

I wonder if I'm ending the day with him.

Impulsively, I pull my phone from my briefcase to take a picture of the sunset; it's just that beautiful, that satisfying to watch after a successful first day at my new job.

But instead of tapping on the camera app, I accidentally

open my photos. I should be focused on the beautiful sight in front of me right now. Yet I find myself watching the video I took that night at Mauna Kea.

When it ends, I touch my fingers to my lips, remembering the kiss we shared just then, how warm his skin felt against mine in that cold wind they have so far up the mountain.

Oh God, I miss him. I miss him so much my heart feels like it's shattered and he's the only glue that will piece me back together again.

But something stirs inside me when I lift my eyes just as the sun falls behind a building in the distance—a feeling of reassurance that something good will come from this love I enjoyed with him, just like my mother told me.

It's up to me to make sure of that.

CHAPTER 23

- DODGER -

"So, Fen tells me you like snorkeling?"

At her question to me, I glance from Amanda—who apparently is my date for the evening—to my brother who sits next to me.

I'm livid with him right now, but I can't show it.

I had thought I was going to dinner with him and his wife. I didn't realize she was bringing her friend along, a move that right now is screaming "set up" to me. And while this woman is quite beautiful, seemingly intelligent, and has even mastered the art of conversation, this is still the last place I want to be right now.

It's unfair to her; my heart is somewhere else.

"I do," I answer her. "Do you do a lot of snorkeling?"

She laughs. "I better. I work on a boat doing tours of Hanauma Bay six times a week."

I have to admit, she's interesting.

"That's how we met," my sister-in-law Kaila interjects. Her eyes light with the pride of knowing that she's managed to find me a date who has some promise. "Fen took me out to Hanauma for our one-month anniversary. And with Amanda's love of the water, I knew you two would hit it off," Kaila finishes.

Ah, so I have Kaila to blame for this.

"One-month anniversary?" I can't help saying, lifting an eyebrow at my brother, wondering at what point couples stop celebrating month anniversaries. "What's planned for the two-month?"

Fen's gaze diverts to his new wife and he gives her a devilish look as he answers me with, "I think we'll be staying in for that one."

God, save me from their marital bliss right now.

I thought this would be a good idea, coming out to Oʻahu to distract myself from Samantha's departure. But watching these two together is possibly the worst medicine for a broken heart.

Because I'm discovering that, while I used to profess that hearts are merely organs for pumping blood, I can't deny that it does ache just there behind my ribcage—especially around midday. That's when I see the sun and picture Samantha on the other side of the world watching the day end without me.

My date glances at me as she stands. "I think I'll run to the ladies' room," she says, grabbing her purse.

"I'll join you," Kaila says.

My brother and I glance at each other as soon as they're out of earshot.

"She's nice, right?" Fen beams. "Seriously, Kaila's got good taste when it comes to picking out dates for you. She spotted her on that boat immediately."

"Fen, why didn't you tell me you were setting me up

tonight? I thought it was just going to be the three of us."

"Oh, come on, Dodger. Kaila hatched the idea and I thought it would be great. I knew you wouldn't come if I told you. Look, she's a hell of a lot better than any of the girls you've managed to find on your own."

"They haven't *all* been that bad."

"Dude, the last time I visited, that girl you were with looked at me and asked me what I would do if all the rain turned into butter. That's not a freaking normal question."

"She was the creative type," I defend, not that I liked the woman either. "Stella used to ask questions like that."

"Stella was four," he deadpans.

"Okay, you're right." I cross my arms. "My dating life has been beyond pathetic lately. But I'm not ready to start dating again."

"It's been almost two months since Hailey left. How cold does the body have to be before we bury it?"

"It's not Hailey on my mind, Fen." My shoulders slump. "I started dating someone and she… left."

Fen winces. "Oh, crap. I'm sorry. Why didn't you tell me? I wouldn't have set this up."

I shrug. "Not much to tell. She went back to DC. Game over."

"Aw, man. Your luck is the pits, dude. How'd you meet her?"

"It was Samantha. Baby K's godmother. Remember her? She was here visiting for ten days." Ten days. The words ring in my head. How could it have only been ten days?

"Sam—yeah, of course I remember her. Not much, though, since she barely ever looked up from—"

"—her cell phone," I interrupt, finishing for him. "Yeah. But when she did finally look up from it… dammit, Fen." I shake my head.

A sly grin slides up my brother's face. "Holy crap. You fell in love with her. In ten days? You fell in love," he repeats as though he's rubbing it in. "Never—*never* would I have expected this from you."

There's a part of me that wants to deny it. But I can't. "That's pretty fucked up, isn't it? I mean, who falls in love in that short a time?"

"Well, aside from your brother?"

My brow furrows. "It hit that quickly for you?"

"You know it did," he reminds me. "You know what it's like? It's like driving down Hawai'i Belt Road back on the Big Island. You can only drive south so far until *BAM!* You're not going anywhere but north up the other side of Hawai'i. There's just no other choice. And you're okay with that."

"You could always turn around," I can't help pointing out.

His face droops. "You know, for such a smart guy, you really should open up your mind a little." Taking a bite of his steak, he pauses. "So what are you going to do about it?"

"What *can* I do about it? She's a lobbyist. Her work is in DC."

"Yeah, and you're a doctor. There are sick people everywhere."

"What do you mean?"

His eyes roll in that devil-may-care way that Fen has about him. "I mean, you loved DC. You know damn well they'd take you again at Walter Reed as a civilian doctor. Hell, that's what Cam and I were betting you'd do when you got out of the Army, anyway. You were happy in that job. Busy, but challenged. Which is more than I can say for you in that urgent care place you started. So if you think you love this girl, you go after her."

"It was a fling."

"That led to something more," he counters.

"I don't even know how she feels about me."

"So, find out." He frowns. "Seriously, Dodger, you keep

thinking that you'll just find someone who will slide right into the life you've built for yourself on the Big Island. And you know what? Keep trying and you might find someone. Like Amanda tonight. She's nice and smart and funny and would probably not mind at all being a doctor's wife and living in a waterfront condo. She could even get a job with some local tour company there. Yet here you are, thinking about someone else. Look, if that doesn't tell you something, nothing will."

I sigh, looking in the distance to where my date disappeared with Kaila. "I feel bad about this. Amanda's actually nice."

"*Coherent* would be a step up for you these days."

I chuckle. "Too true."

He slices a hand through the air dismissively. "Don't worry about Amanda. There's a guy I work with who'd be perfect for her. Better surfer than you, too."

I narrow my eyes. "Hey, now that's getting personal, Fen."

"If the shoe fits, Bro."

I find myself staring at the empty seat in front of me and wishing it was filled with Samantha. "I can't just uproot my life like that, Fen."

"Why the hell not?"

I angle a look at him. "So you expect me to just show up in DC after only being with her for ten days and say, 'Hey, it's been fun. Let's get married.'"

His eyes saucer-wide, Fen's back straightens. "Holy shit. I was just thinking you could maybe give it a test run. I never said anything about marrying her." His grin expands to the point of consuming his face. "But I'm totally loving your idea. Kaila would go positively apeshit if she heard any of this."

"I was kidding, Fen," I lie because honestly, when the words slipped out of my mouth, they felt like the most natural thing I've said since Samantha left. "No one does that."

He shrugs. "Some people do. I mean, why not? When you love someone, it's worth a little risk—you know, throwing your heart out there like that. Even if you were joking about it, it says something that the idea would even cross your mind." He narrows his eyes on me. "But you wouldn't do it. Too damn logical about everything."

He says it like an insult, like I'm a guy who kicks puppies or steals from the collection plate at a church.

After we finish dinner, I walk Amanda to her car and apologize, explaining why my heart just isn't in this date. Her grin is warm and accepting, with eyes that seem to exude that aloha spirit that makes these islands famous.

She gives me a platonic hug good-bye, echoing Fen's sentiment that I should tell Samantha how I feel.

I stand in the parking lot watching her as she drives away. I might be a fool to let this one go. Logic would tell me that she checks all the boxes on my list.

But I'm starting to realize that logic doesn't determine who we should spend our lives with. Destiny—I shudder as the word flits through my brain—might just have a certain someone picked out for each of us, and I get very little say in the matter.

The only question is what I plan to do about it.

Back at Fen's place, I look at my small suitcase that rests on the sofa bed where I'm sleeping, with just enough clothes to hold me over for the handful of days I planned on spending here.

It's insane—this idea that's sparking in my head.

It was just a joke when I had said it to Fen. An extreme exaggeration meant to show him how ridiculous it is that I've even fallen this hard in so little time for a woman who lives on the other side of the world.

Or was I really joking when I said it?

I step onto their lanai and look out into the night. It's not as dark here as it is on the Big Island. Their little house in Kapolei is close to plenty of shopping and tourist attractions.

And jewelry stores. I'll admit I recall seeing a couple of those down near the Four Seasons Resort.

Insane.

I've always been the logical one of the Sheridan brothers, just like Fen said. Hands down, I'd be the least likely to actually do something as crazy as what I'm considering right now. It doesn't make any sense that I'd fall in love with Samantha.

It makes even less sense that I'd want to propose marriage —a lifelong commitment—to someone I've been with for only ten days.

Then I think of Amanda tonight, and every woman I might date in the future who meets all the damn criteria that I've got drafted up in my brain. And how none of them—*none* —will ever make me feel as complete as I do when I'm with Samantha.

There's nothing logical about that. But it's the only truth I know.

I never should have let her leave without telling her I love her.

I never should have thought that it was *her* role to fit into my life, without being ready to do the same for her.

I never should have questioned that the thing that holds my brothers' marriages so tightly together is something that I simply can't explain with all my logic and rationalization, or my endless supply of scientific analogies and medical jargon.

And even though I'll swear to my dying day that love is just the right cocktail of neurotransmitters stirring in the brain, maybe there's one ingredient in there that I haven't accounted for until right now.

An ingredient like destiny.

If that's not reason enough to risk making a complete ass of myself, then I don't know what is.

CHAPTER 24

~ SAMANTHA ~

I almost don't want to go tonight.

After just a few days home now, my old tradition of watching my sunsets from the Capitol building seems somehow hollow to me, even with a crystal clear evening promising a sunset that is worthy of a postcard.

I don't want a repeat of last night or the one before that. I don't want that ache, that emptiness that I feel as soon as I step out of my office and my focus shifts from work... to Dodger.

These first days in my new job have been the kind that should make me feel validated, important, and confident that coming back to DC was the right thing to do. But when I watch the sun set, picturing the way its warm rays are shining down on Dodger so far from me, all I feel is a longing for something I simply can't have.

My phone chirps in my pocket, reminding me that even

after only being away from my office for a matter of minutes, already there are texts and emails that need my attention. That used to be enough to please me.

Yet I don't reach for it as quickly as I used to.

I turn onto Pennsylvania Avenue and see the Capitol in the distance, such a grand, intimidating building. At this time of day, it somehow manages to look inviting in the warm evening glow. I'm not sure I'll even stop there tonight, but I have to walk past it anyway to reach my apartment. So I continue down the familiar path toward home.

Work should fill my mind. It should edge out the memories of Dodger and force me to live in the here and now. And every sunset should fill my heart the same way it used to.

But sunsets belong to Dodger now.

I stop momentarily in the middle of the sidewalk, cursing inwardly before I resume my fast pace.

There's nothing practical about falling in love with a man who's on an island in the middle of the ocean, or so my brain is shouting at me right now.

But then my heart whispers to me something completely different.

You should have told him how you feel, it seems to say, a tiny voice coming from just inside that ache in my chest. A stupid idea entirely. Telling him how I feel after just ten days together would have been a huge misstep, making things awkward for me every time I visit my precious goddaughter in the future.

Dodger boasts about being logical the same way I used to say I was eternally practical. He couldn't possibly feel as deeply for me as I do for him.

As I approach the base of the building, I keep my toes pointed in the direction home. But then nostalgia tugs at me.

I'll do this, just one more time, if only to prove to myself that I really can watch the sunset without crying for an hour when I get home afterward.

Next week, I'll start a new evening tradition. Something that has no link to Dodger. Maybe I'll volunteer at the food bank or start taking nightly walks through Eastern Market where the lively atmosphere is bound to distract me from memories.

Or maybe I'll take up rowing and join one of those clubs I see on the Potomac so that my heart will be pumping just hard enough to remind me that the damn thing is still functioning, despite the fact that it's split in two.

Maybe. But tonight, I'm drawn to the steps one more time.

I glance over my shoulder at the sun as I approach the building, then trudge up the steps, barely looking up. Barely... until I catch a glimpse of someone who looks eerily like...

Dodger?

Oh, wow. I must still be jetlagged.

I quickly glance away, not wanting to stare, and I continue up the stairs. But then I hear my name.

"Samantha."

I stop and look at the man about twenty steps away from me now. The sun is at my back, so there should be no need to squint. Yet still I do as my brain scrambles for some explanation for what I'm seeing.

"Dodger?"

Then his smile appears and I know I've lost my mind, watching him walk down a handful of stairs toward me.

"Dodger?" I repeat. My voice is too quiet for him to hear me. It's more to myself than to him.

"Hey..." His voice trails as he reaches me and then touches my hand. And just like that, the void again is filled.

Just like that.

Mouth gaping, I stare at him, until shock gets edged out by sheer confusion. "What—what are you doing here?"

He gives a little shrug. "Well, I got to share my favorite sunset with you on Mauna Kea. I thought maybe I should come here and see how yours measures up by comparison." His smile fades a little. "Is that all right? I guess I should have called or texted. But I took the chance that I'd find you here."

"No—I mean, yes. Yes, it's all right. This is such a surprise. I guess I'm just... stunned. I thought you were with Fen on O'ahu right now."

"I was. Until I realized there was something I needed to tell you."

He pauses, just long enough that I feel compelled to point out, "You can always call me."

His smile returns. "Some things need a—what was it you said once to me? A grand gesture, I think you called it that morning on my lanai. But I recall you told me there should be a horse involved and a ride into the sunset." He looks over his shoulder. "I, uh, couldn't get the permit for the horse, though."

I cock my head, vaguely remembering something I said like that, but still wondering what the heck he's talking about. Holding up my hands, I offer a little shrug. "I'm sorry. But I'm a little lost here."

"Perfect transition for me," he says, confusing me further. "Because I've been lost, too. Since you left, that is. I feel like I've got a piece of me missing when you're not near."

There's a sudden moisture in my eyes, just hearing him say to me what I've been feeling in my heart since I last touched him.

"I love you, Samantha," he goes on to say, as I let a tear fall. "I should have told you that at the airport before you left. I thought I was doing the right thing for you by not saying it. Because as much as I wanted you to stay, I also wanted you to leave. I wanted you to start this new job and let it be everything you'd dreamed about. I wanted that for you."

"I love you, too, Dodger." I breathe out the confession, feeling nothing but relief to release the words from my soul. "I didn't want to tell you because I know you'll find someone on that island who will be a perfect fit in your life."

"I already found that person. It's you, Samantha. And I know that packing up and moving for a woman after just ten days together sounds crazy and irrational, but I've made DC my home before, and I can do it again. For you, I'd do that. I'd do anything."

I feel the tears on my cheeks. "But you have a clinic back on the Big Island, Dodger. You have a life there. You can't just leave that."

"Watch me," he says with boyish enthusiasm. "I've already contacted my partners and told them I'd be interested in selling them my share of the clinic. And I've emailed a few colleagues at Walter Reed where I used to work, asking them about starting a job there as a civilian doctor. But if they can't find a place for me, I'll find something else. I don't care what it is, Samantha. So long as I'm with you."

I open my mouth to say something, though I'm not even sure what. I want him here—desperately. But I picture his home there in paradise and his brothers so close by and I can't possibly imagine him giving all that up for me.

"Wait—" He holds up his hand. "Don't say anything yet." He backs onto the step just beneath me, then angles himself so he can go down on one knee.

His grin is sheepish. "I didn't realize how awkward it is to kneel on steps until just now."

"What are you doing?" I gasp.

He reaches into his pocket and pulls out a small box. When he opens it, the last rays of the sun sparkle inside the diamond.

"I'm asking you to be my wife. I know it's crazy to do this after ten days. And this is the last thing I'd ever picture a guy like me doing. But that's because I never knew a woman like you existed. I *never* thought I'd fall in love like this—"

His voice is adamant, as though he's discovering it again right now in front of me.

"—so completely," he continues. "And if you want a long engagement or if you even want to delay this conversation for a while, I understand. But dammit, I've led my entire life doing the logical thing and this time I want to defy that guy I used to be. You've changed me, Samantha. There's no going back to who I was before."

"Dodger, I—I don't want you to have to uproot your life like that. I could—" *move to Hawai'i*, I'm about to say, because just then I realize I could do that. I could chuck a career I love to follow a man I love *more*.

But he cuts me off.

"Marry me?" he says like a question. "That's how I'm hoping you were going to finish that sentence. You could… marry me?"

Chills blanket every square inch of my skin. Because I could marry him. Because it's the practical thing to do when I love a man so completely.

And I'm a practical kind of girl.

"Yes, Dodger. I could marry you. And I *will* marry you."

He slips the ring on my finger, and rises to his full height, taking me in his arms. I hear a smattering of applause from some of the other people who share these steps with us, watching the sunset.

Yet the sound of it seems so distant, as though right now, Dodger and I are on our own island, far from the rest of the world as he touches his lips to mine and fills my heart completely.

EPILOGUE

EIGHT MONTHS LATER

- DODGER -

"Cam here thinks we should buy a vacation rental property on the Big Island."

Standing here on my lanai for the last time, I could swear I hear Fen's voice as clear as I did that day so many years ago. It seems to be a whisper on the breeze, just loud enough that I can still hear it above the sound of the surf breaking in front of me.

"Why?" I had asked him.

"Dodger, look at this place. It's freakin' paradise. Who wouldn't want a piece of this?"

"You were so right, little brother," I can't help saying right now, all alone as I stare out to the ocean.

All alone, except for the palms swaying in the wind and a whale that breaches in the distance reminding me that it's winter here in Hawai'i.

I remember telling Samantha about that—sitting right out here in the darkness. Telling her all about how we mark the change of seasons here, just before I kissed her for the first time.

So many memories here.

This was the place where my brothers and I made our home after the Army, each of them selling their own share in it to me when they married their wives.

Yet it's still our place together to me. Even though it's my signature alone that will be needed to transfer ownership of this place today. This is Sheridan domain, the place where we bonded as brothers and became the kind of men who could place our hearts in the care of the women we love.

This place is special to me. I couldn't let it go without attending this real estate closing in person, even though my agent told me I don't have to be here. Even if it does mean flying 4,500 miles at a time when I should be at home, helping Samantha finalize the details for our upcoming wedding.

Still, even she knew I needed to come.

Either that, or she wanted me to butt out of the wedding plans. Yeah, that's more likely the case, I consider as a warm smile touches my cheeks.

It doesn't help me to know that the person who's buying my condo is doing it through some bogus "nominee"—which tells me that it's probably some international company who's buying up properties around here to rent them out.

I'd rather picture a real person here, hanging up their

framed photos on the wall and making their mark on this island the same way my brothers and I did.

Or better still, I'd love to imagine a family settling down here, maybe a couple little kids running out the door to the beach and then tracking piles of sand in on their feet hours later.

I'm kicking myself for accepting the full-price offer without looking into it harder. But between juggling a full patient load at Walter Reed and planning a wedding, it was easy to let it fall off my radar screen. So now I have to face the prospect of my place—*our* place—being taken over by some faceless corporate entity.

I expel a long breath and turn on my heel to go inside to lock up.

I should have just kept the place. I could have afforded it. I sold my share of the urgent care clinic here, but kept a stake in the company I created, as well as its Maui franchise and the new one that opened on Kaua'i. That alone is pulling in enough money to cover the added expense of keeping this place.

But owning a property 4,500 miles away comes with its share of headaches. And right now, I want to build a life and a family in DC—something that I'm sure will come with a fair share of headaches itself down the road. With luck, in years to come, I'll be dealing with playdates, long nights helping with school projects, and eventually—God help me—teen angst and raging hormones because I'm sure my brothers and I put my own parents through hell and it's bound to come around full circle.

Those are the things that will need my full attention, I remind myself as I get in my rental car. Not some property on the other side of the world which I'm reluctant to let go.

The drive to the settlement agency in Kona only takes about a half hour. Traffic is scarce as it usually is here on the

Big Island, at least compared to my new home smack dab in the middle of Capitol Hill.

Samantha and I have settled into a brownstone that we're renovating room by room in our spare time, not that there will be much of that till after the wedding. In truth, even though I feel a pinch in my heart being here right now and not calling the Big Island "home" any longer, I'm happier than I've ever been with my new life. My job is continually challenging, but I've managed to find the balance that I lacked the last time I lived in DC.

Samantha has been the key to that. We've even joined a rowing club and it's been fun starting a new hobby together while getting our fill of the water. She's thriving in her career and I'm back to feeling like I'm making a difference in my patients' lives, something I missed at the urgent care clinic here on the island.

I pause for a moment after I park the car. There's a part of me that doesn't want to go into the building because I know what I'll see. Not some anxious couple ready to take the keys to my place and make it their own—but instead, some slick businessperson who has no stake in my home whatsoever—just a representative of a company poised to profit from renting out the place.

I hate this.

I open the door and identify myself to the receptionist, and my real estate agent comes out to meet me with an odd look on her face.

"This isn't quite protocol," she begins. "But the buyers would like to meet with you alone first."

"Alone?"

"Um, yes. It's not—well, do you mind?" She looks as confused as I am.

I shrug with annoyance. It's not like I need someone at my side anyway. "Fine with me."

She leads me toward a conference room. When she opens the door, my brow furrows at what I see.

"What the hell are you two doing here?" I blurt at my brothers, confused beyond belief.

They're both laughing, probably at the look on my face. But I'm finding nothing amusing about any of this. While there's a sliver of me that appreciates them showing up—I assume to show me support as I let go of a place we once shared together —I'd rather face doing this alone. Just get it over with, not sit here and be reminded of the memories we made at our condo before I sign it over to whomever next shows up in this room.

"Dodger," Cam speaks first. "*We're* the buyers."

"What?"

"We're the buyers," Fen repeats my brother's words.

Confused, I pull out a chair and sit. *The buyers would like to meet with you alone first,* I'm remembering my agent saying.

"You're the buyers?" I feel the need to confirm, then glancing over at the stack of paperwork. "That was *your* offer I signed?"

Cam chuckles. "Yeah, that was us."

I'm shaking my head. "Why didn't you tell me?"

"Because," Fen says, "we wanted to make sure you got a fair price. And if we told you we wanted the place back, you would have given it to us."

"I would have made you pay *more*," I scoff because that's what's expected of me, even though what he says is probably true.

"Yeah, right. There was that risk, too," Cam jokes right back at me.

I shake my head. "But you two have homes of your own. Why do you want the condo?"

They shrug in unison.

"It's *ours*, Dodger," Fen says. "It's where we—I don't know

—got the Army out of our bloodstream and moved onto the next stage in our lives, you know?"

I know. I know too well.

"We couldn't see the place going to someone else. It's for Sheridans. And why the hell shouldn't we have our own beachfront place we can offer out to family when they visit, you know? We're doing well enough."

My gaze moves from Cam to Fen, then back to Cam. I feel better somehow, knowing that our condo meant the same thing to them as it did to me.

I narrow my eyes. "Okay. I'll sell it to you. On one condition."

Fen straightens in his chair. "Hey, no conditions. We've got your signature on these papers already, you know."

"Don't get stubborn with me, Fenway." I use his full name on purpose because I know he hates that. And that's what brothers do. "I'll sell a third of it to each of you. But no more than that."

Cam's expression is cautious. "Who gets the final third?"

"Me," I say. "I want in on this. And Samantha and I can use it when we visit."

Cam's face morphs into that stubborn one I used to see a lot when he was a kid. "Dodger, we can afford it on our own. We don't need your help, you know."

"I'm well aware of that. But it would piss me off to think of you guys owning it without me."

Fen grins. "I like this. The *other* Sheridans own vacation properties. Why the hell can't we?"

The other Sheridans. The words jostle loose a memory of us on the beach when we first got the idea of buying our place together.

It's Fen's voice in my head again like it was when I was just out on my lanai earlier this afternoon. And I'm recalling the three of us sitting in the powder-soft sand along the shores of Kaua'i at my cousin's wedding.

"We can make our own name for ourselves out here," he had said that evening, so many years ago when we were all still in the Army. *"Not be the* other *Sheridans."*

Now, I realize how young we must have sounded back then, so anxious to distinguish ourselves from our family name.

Cam's voice brings me back to the present. "We can rent it out when it's not in use like we did before."

"Or better yet, maybe offer it up for free to Soldiers we know who might need some time away with their families," Fen adds.

I grin, thinking of the ones I see every day at Walter Reed who could benefit from a dose of paradise. "Now you're talking my language."

Fen leans forward in his chair, his grin widening. "Besides, we're going to have family visiting even more next year."

"Why's that?" I ask Fen as he shares a conspiring look with my other brother.

He reaches for the folder with the settlement papers and opens it. Then I see the sonogram on the top of the stack. "It's a boy. Meet Dodger Camden Sheridan."

Holy crap. My eyes take in the image. A nephew. I'm going to be an uncle again to…

Wait a second.

"Dodger Camden Sheridan?" I ask, unable to stop the cringe that forms on my face.

Two harsh lines form on Cam's brow. "Hey, Fen, you told me your son was going to be *Camden Dodger* Sheridan," he protests, changing the order of the name.

I'm still frowning at the sonogram.

Name his son after baseball stadiums like our dad did? Seriously? After all the hell we went through for that as kids?

I gaze at the black-and-white image of my unsuspecting nephew who is right now growing inside my sister-in-law's belly. *Don't worry, little guy. I've got your back.*

"He'll be neither one," I say adamantly. "You'll give this kid a normal name, or I'll tear up this contract and sell my place to the next buyer that comes along."

Fen's eyes turn to slits. "You wouldn't dare."

"Damn right I would, *Fenway*. I know you thought your name was the worst of the three, but I'm telling you, after hearing 'Roger, Dodger' from kids for the first eighteen years of my life, I can say that at least *Fenway* doesn't rhyme with anything."

He holds up his hands. "Okay, okay. We'll name our boy after Kaila's dad. She'd probably like that."

"What was his name?"

"Ikaika. It's Hawaiian."

Cam lets out a chuckle. "Well, that sure doesn't rhyme with anything."

Ikaika. "What's it mean?" I ask.

"Someone who's strong," Fen answers.

"Well, with you as his dad, he'll need that," Cam snorts.

I laugh with my brother, even though it's the furthest thing from the truth.

This kid will be strong, but he won't need it. Not for a long time. Because he has us.

And Sheridans look out for each other.

FROM THE AUTHOR

Thank you so much for reading *Island Fever*! If you enjoyed the story of Dodger and Samantha, I hope you'll take a moment to leave a review. Five-star reviews truly do sell books, bringing me closer to the day when I might be able to give up my "day job" and do this full time. So I'm deeply grateful for them.

I always hate saying good-bye to characters. So, from time to time, I often revisit the places and people in my books and write free bonus scenes that I love to share with my readers. Please check my website at www.KateAster.com/bonuses to see my latest.

Also, if you haven't quite gotten your fill of the Sheridans, be sure to read the original series, HOMEFRONT: THE SHERIDANS. And I promise you that you'll have lots of opportunities to check in on your old friends in my future books. Be sure to sign up at my website at www.KateAster.com so that I can email you the moment my newest books are available.

My endless thanks to my *'ohana* in Hawai'i. I could not have written this book without your technical help, ensuring I properly used my *'okina*—even if it *does* get mutilated in some e-reader formats—and (hopefully) spelled all those beautiful Hawaiian words correctly. And my apologies for not using the *kahako* above vowels in a few instances. I tried to, but sadly, e-readers won't recognize them.

A big shout-out to one of my favorite charities, **808 Cleanups** (www.808cleanups.org), who work so hard to keep Hawaiʻi's beaches clean. If you are ever lucky enough to visit paradise, I encourage you to give back to the island that gives to us and spend a day on the beach with some of their wonderful volunteers if you are able.

As always, my special thanks to my husband for all his Army expertise... this series was for you, my love. And to Danielle for your sharp eyes and irreplaceable friendship.

Most of all, my thanks go to my readers. You are my cheering squad. Any time I think I can't handle juggling motherhood with a full-time job, and then still write romance on the side, I hear from one of you and it inspires me to keep at it! Thank you for being so supportive!

I LOVE to hear from readers. Feel free to drop me a line through my website at www.KateAster.com, and you'll be the first to hear when my next book is available for release.

BOOKS BY KATE ASTER

~ SPECIAL OPS: HOMEFRONT SERIES~

Romance awaits and life-long friendships blossom
on the shores of the Chesapeake Bay.

———

SEAL the Deal

Special Ops: Homefront (Book One)

The SEAL's Best Man

Special Ops: Homefront (Book Two)

Contract with a SEAL

Special Ops: Homefront (Book Three)

Make Mine a Ranger

Special Ops: Homefront (Book Four)

BOOKS BY KATE ASTER

~ SPECIAL OPS: TRIBUTE SERIES~

Love gets a second chance when a very special ice cream shop
opens near the United States Naval Academy.

———————

No Reservations

Special Ops: Tribute (Book One)

Strong Enough

Special Ops: Tribute (Book Two)

Until Forever: A Wedding Novella

Special Ops: Tribute (Book Three)

Twice Tempted

Special Ops: Tribute (Book Four)

BOOKS BY KATE ASTER

~ HOMEFRONT: THE SHERIDANS SERIES ~

When one fledgling dog rescue comes along, three brothers find romance as they emerge from the shadow of their billionaire name.

More, Please

Homefront: The Sheridans (Book One)

Full Disclosure

Homefront: The Sheridans (Book Two)

Faking It

Homefront: The Sheridans (Book Three)

BOOKS BY KATE ASTER

~ HOMEFRONT: ALOHA, SHERIDANS SERIES ~

Even on a remote island paradise, a handful of bachelor brothers
can't hide from love when they leave the Army.

A is for Alpha

Homefront: Aloha, Sheridans (Book One)

Hindsight

Homefront: Aloha, Sheridans (Book Two)

Island Fever

Homefront: Aloha, Sheridans (Book Three)

BOOKS BY KATE ASTER

~ BROTHERS IN ARMS SERIES ~

With two U.S. Naval Academy graduates and two from their arch
rival at West Point, there's ample discord among the Adler brothers
… until love tames them.

————————

BFF'ed

Brothers in Arms (Book One) - available now!

Books Two, Three, and Four
are coming soon.

*Sign up at my website at **www.KateAster.com***
to be the first to hear the release dates.

BOOKS BY KATE ASTER

~ FIRECRACKERS: NO COMMITMENT
NOVELETTES ~

For when you don't have much free time... but want a quick, fun

race to a happily ever after.

———————

SEAL My Grout

Firecrackers: No Commitment Novelettes (Book One)

Available now!

Novelettes Two, Three, and Four

are coming soon.

*Sign up at my website at **www.KateAster.com***

to be the first to hear the release dates.

LET'S KEEP IN TOUCH!

Twitter: @KateAsterAuthor

Facebook: @KateAsterAuthor

Instagram: KateAsterAuthor

www.KateAster.com

Made in the USA
Columbia, SC
18 October 2020